DRIVING FORCE

THE DRIVING SERIES
BOOK ONE

HALEY COOK

SOUTHERN LIBRARIAN PUBLISHING

Formatting by HC PA & Formatting Services

Cover Design by Sammie Bee Designs

Cadwallader Photography

Model: Aaron Wolber

Editing by Kate Segers

ISBN: 9798395476562 (paperback)

ISBN: 9798851734946 (hardback)

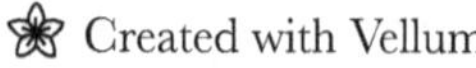 Created with Vellum

DRIVING Force

HALEY COOK

CONTENTS

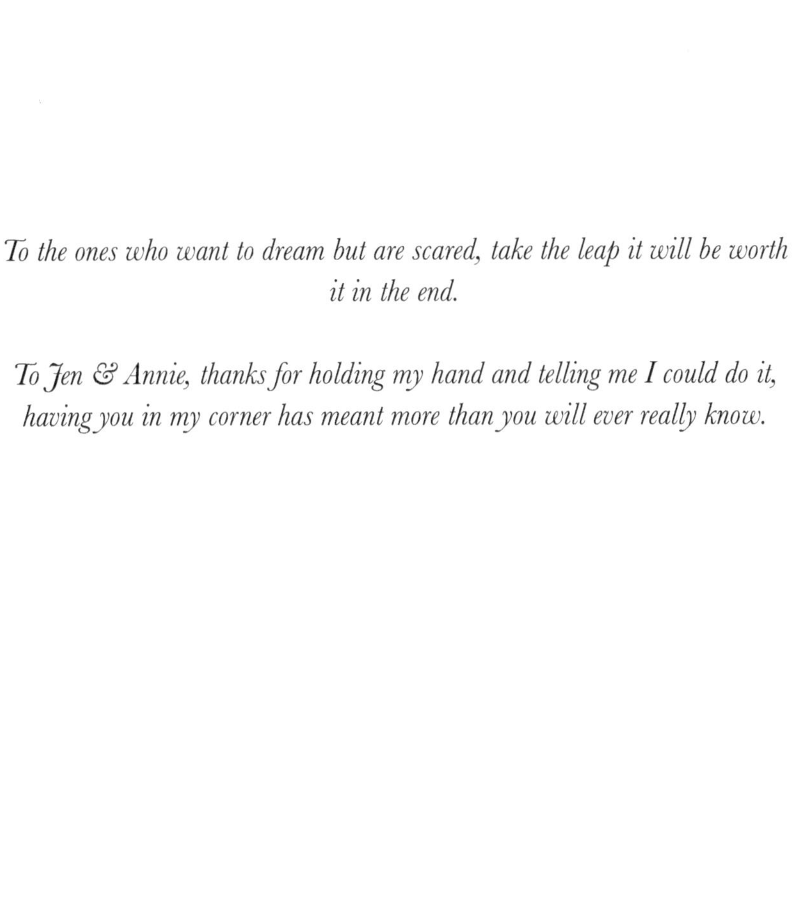

To the ones who want to dream but are scared, take the leap it will be worth it in the end.

To Jen & Annie, thanks for holding my hand and telling me I could do it, having you in my corner has meant more than you will ever really know.

Chapter 1
Tinley

"Y'all—I DO NOT WANT TO GO!"

Ignoring my protest, I'm thrust into the shower. "You're going—kicking and screaming if that's what we have to do," Mia declares. Having been my best friend since freshman year at App State, she knows when it's time to get me out of the house. "You need a day out away from books and working at that library surrounded by more books. It's your last year. Enjoy college for a change."

What's wrong with liking books? I think to myself.

"Tin, I know what's rolling around in that little head of yours, and yes, books are fine, but you need other things in your life. Like boys and boys and more boys," she points out.

"Mia, you know I'm the girl who is invisible to boys or the one they friend zone, right? I may be the quiet girl, but I'm not as shy as some may think. I just don't let people get too close because I don't want my heart broken."

"That's where you're wrong, Tin. You just don't let them see you and the awesome person you are because you have read so many romance novels that no man can ever live up to that idea of the perfect partner."

It's easy for her to say. Her dark brown hair, big blue eyes, and curvy figure make the boys stop and take notice anywhere we go.

"Ugh. Okay, fine, I'll go." I give in, but my less-than-pleased tone makes my reluctance very clear.

Living with my best friends for the past three years, I understand that we usually have the most fun when they get me out of my comfort zone. Mia, Grace, Lily, and I might be very close, but you build a complex quickly when you're the single girl and everyone else is coupled up. I can't help if I get lost in my studies more than hanging out with the six of them. My Saturday nights usually consist of the girls getting ready for dates and me reading the latest book on my Kindle instead of being the seventh wheel.

And yes, I know what you're thinking - *Don't they have hot friends to set you up with to go along with them?* The answer is yes, they do, considering they are all dating guys on the baseball team. But their guy friends always seem to see me as the chubby girl who makes them laugh, not girlfriend material. Don't get me wrong, they have all been super sweet, but it's always the same thing. "I like you, but I just think we are off as better friends." So, it never goes further than the first date.

If they are dragging me to God knows what today, I better put some effort into it, or I'll, as my mother says, *die alone with a cat*—by the way, I don't even like cats—then it'll eat my face off. Since I'm alone, no one will find me until it's too late. Insert face palm emoji here, please.

After finally pulling myself out of the shower and drying off, I'm met with three pairs of eyes staring at me like I'd just said I was Team Jacob instead of Team Edward.

"Umm, ladies, what's up?" I no sooner get the last word out before different clothing options are thrust at me like I've never dressed myself before.

"Okay, let's slow down. Of course, I have some questions. First," I lift my hand, "where are we going? And second, why are all three of you so excited about this?"

Lily is the first to chime in. She's usually the quieter of the four of us, the normal southern girl. Auburn red hair, dark green eyes, and the sweetest personality you will ever meet. Even if she told me she planned to kill me in my sleep, she's so sweet I wouldn't believe it until it happened. This explains how she landed James, the star baseball player, two years ago. We are all sure she'll follow him to whichever farm team he lands at after the draft in a few months.

"Ok, so don't kill us, but we're going to a NASCAR race," Lily tells me, a little too excited for my taste.

Pausing to let it sink in a little, I finally reply, "Umm, y'all know I like quiet places, right? I mean, I work in a library and want to go into publishing when I finish school. In what universe did you think this would scream, 'Hey, Tin will love this and will put up no struggle whatsoever about going?'" I ask, looking at them quizzically.

"Yeah, yeah, we know you like boring," Grace chimes in.

Yes, Grace is that friend, that bitchy girl that will always say what she thinks even if no one wants to hear it. She has blonde hair, green eyes, and wears her signature red lipstick, ready to cut any man who might impede her because she gets what she wants.

"But guess what, Tin? You're going! I pulled some strings, and a family friend who does PR for a team is letting me get some experience for my PR/Social Media class. He got us all passes to the Food City 500 Race in Bristol, Tennessee since it's only an hour from here."

Knowing I don't really have a choice, I shrug. "I better get dressed, then. Yee haw, make me a NASCAR pit lizard, I guess. Show me what I've been missing all these years."

None of my friends find my sarcasm or exaggerated Southern accent funny. Instead, they pounce on me like lions in the jungle that just found their last meal. When they finally give me an inch of breathing room, I turn to look at myself. The dark colors of the royal blue fitted tee and dark-washed jeans enhance my curvy figure, but my favorite part is the signature sparkly chucks that I always wear.

"Let the games begin, bitches!"

Grace does her Breakfast Club fist bump in the air. Lily stands back, jumping and clapping, and Mia just shouts, "Hell yeah, you are smoking hot!"

I don't know about smoking hot, but I feel better than average with my hair done in loose curls and a little makeup applied. The humidity living in North Carolina can be rough, so it's best to just go natural.

Going to a race might be the craziest idea known to man because I know I'll be out of my element. But my girls have all the confidence in the world, making me smile and hold my head higher. Just as we walk into the living room, a knock comes from the front door. Lily heads toward it like she has a beacon on James and knows his every move–but I've always been told that it's the quiet ones you've got to watch out for.

James no more gets his foot in the door than I realize I'm once again the seventh wheel. Lily and James are so cute it would make anyone sick. When James settled down, his buddies wanted that same thing, so that's how Mia and Grace fell for his best friends. Here I sit, a single girl in a room full of couples. Then, out of the corner of my eye, I notice a guy I haven't seen before trailing behind Miles. Granted, it's hard to see around Miles. Standing six foot three and built like a linebacker, he takes up a lot of space. James is the shortest of the bunch by a few inches. It's hard not to look at them and see why my best friends are lucky women. Internally kicking myself for being so picky. Great, not only am I going to a sporting event I know nothing about, but now I'm being set up on a blind date. Yep, where is the wormhole I can jump in?

"Okay, are we ready to go? I need to see what the huge deal is with NASCAR."

Miles, Grace's boyfriend, is the first to chime in. "You're going to love it, Tin. Fast cars and beer. What's not to love?"

"Miles, you know me so well." *Just kill me now,* is what I really mean, but I give him a playful smile.

The next thing I know, James is pushing a handsome man with blonde hair and light green eyes in front of me. If I were a betting woman, I'd say this is one of his athlete friends based on his build alone.

"Tinley, this is Chase, and no, he does not play any sports before you even ask. Well, not at school, anyway. I know you're tired of athletes. Even though I should be hurt by that, I'm not. He's in my sports medicine class."

"Hi, Tinley." Chase reaches out to shake my hand. "It's nice to meet you. James has told me a lot about you. Thanks for letting me tag along to the race today."

Lordy, this man is nice to look at. His sea-green eyes could make a girl lose all train of thought and whereabouts when his attention is on them. Maybe it won't be such a bad day after all. "It's nice to meet you, Chase. I would love to say that James and Lily have also told me all about you," I laugh a little, "but they didn't. I'm so sorry."

"Well, if I had known that James had such a beautiful friend, I would have made sure he had given me your contact sooner." I can't help but blush at the statement. Chase may just be what I was looking for, or maybe he could help me figure out this racing shit my friends thought I needed to understand.

As we follow the others out and load up into Miles's suburban, I tell myself to just enjoy today. Even if it kills me. And between NASCAR and a blind date, it just might.

Chapter 2
Ryan

Being at the racetrack is one of the best parts of my week; the smell of gas and tires, the crews preparing to go to work on pitstops, and the rush of adrenaline that hits when I get in the car, but this morning I'm met with Brad in my race hauler at the ass crack of dawn. "Why do I have to play nice with a college student studying Public Relations? Aren't they supposed to have an internship program for that?" I question my PR guy Brad while buttoning my jeans and throwing on an old racing shirt and dark gray vans.

Brad met me at my racing hauler to give me the rundown of what needed to be done for the day from a drivers' meet and greet, which I enjoy since it's a time to talk with the fans. The drivers' pre-race meeting afterwards is the one time of the day away from the public eye. After that, the always-important interview with NASCAR Race Day, and then hopefully ending with the victory lane hat dance, yet with how the car ran yesterday, I'm going to have to bust my ass to make that one happen.

Brad blows out a frustrated breath. "Yes, they have internship programs, but this is a family friend, and I told her it would be a great chance to see if this is the sport she wants to cover once she graduates school in May."

Okay. I take a deep breath. *I'll be good as gold today and try not to make life difficult.* Normally, I'm a nice guy at the track once you get past the sometimes-grumpy part, which I blame on no coffee or lack of sleep most days. But when the moment comes, and my helmet is on, I turn into the NASCAR superstar Ryan McKenzie and will do anything to win. That would explain why I've made a few enemies on the circuit and have Brad attached to my hip anytime I'm at the track, but it comes with the territory when you win races.

"So, when will she be here?" Ready to get this show underway as we walk toward my meet and greet. I have always loved coming to the track early. The smell of the cars when they first crank and the burnt rubber of tires lingering in the air from the night before has always made me smile. "Could be anytime, really."

He no more gets the sentence out, when a group of college-age adults walks up to us. NASCAR was always my end goal, so I skipped college and went straight to the Xfinity series from high school. I was lucky to have signed with Mac Motorsports early in my career, getting on NASCAR's radar when I started racing midgets. They were good to me, and I was a loyal driver. So, when I could, I moved up the ranks and entered the big show a few years later. I have never taken that for granted because I know it does not happen to everyone so quickly.

Walking toward the first meet and greet, Brad is rattling off the stats for this track and who's lining up where when a tall blonde comes up to me, drawing my attention. But as soon as she opens her mouth, I sense she only sees me as a driver to put on her Instagram page and claim she's slept with.

"Ryan, I'm such a big fan," she purrs.

"Thanks so much for the support, but I'm late for an event." I pull her hand away from my bicep. Don't get me wrong, sometimes it's nice to have female attention, but my coffee hasn't even kicked this early in the morning, so it's a bit over the top for me.

"Ah, come on, driver." She winks. "I can make your morning even better," she whispers in my ear as I pull away to continue my walk.

Glancing at the group headed toward us, I can't help but think back about my friends in high school and how close we had been once, but we soon drifted apart when I found racing. That was my true passion, and going headfirst into it, I lost them along the way, but I never looked back.

Brad greets everyone, getting names and ensuring they can access the garage area to watch the race from the stands or behind the pit wall. Fans stopped me, so I missed everyone's names. When you have a ridiculously cute nine-year-old with your t-shirt on and her dad asking you to sign something, you do not turn them down. Making my way over to Brad, I notice a beautiful blonde standing beside him, and I can't help but take a moment and admire her.

"Ryan McKenzie, this is Grace. Grace, this is Ryan."

"Umm, bud, my eyes are up here," Grace says with a smug smile.

I can't help but laugh a little, getting caught looking at all of Grace's curves. Then I catch a glimpse of another woman out of the corner of my eye, with the most beautiful, dark, midnight black curls I have ever seen and crystal blue eyes hiding behind the cutest pair of black frame glasses. I shake my head and smile to myself. Normally, glasses don't catch my attention, but something about these makes me look a little longer than necessary.

Clearing my throat, I tell Grace, "Sorry about that," just as the dark-haired beauty turns away from me.

"So Brad tells me you have a full morning with promotion, including a meet and greet before the race. Are you sure it's okay if I follow you guys around?" Grace asks.

"Yeah, it's just a normal race day for me. Brad said you wanted to work in NASCAR, so why not see what it's all about?"

As I go over all that's expected of me on race day, those crystal blue eyes grab my attention again, and it makes my heart rate pick up just a little as she walks up to Grace. Before I can even think, I reach out, wanting to touch her hand.

"Um, hi. I'm Ryan, and you are?" I know I must have startled her, but I can't let her walk away without getting her name at least. She stands there for a second, looking like she's trying to solve a math problem, which makes me laugh a little to myself. Then I wondered how it was possible men didn't approach her and say hello on a regular basis. She is one of the most beautiful women I have ever seen, and the way she carries herself, she doesn't even seem to realize that.

As a driver, girls always come and go, yet no one holds my attention for longer than a few weeks, if that. But something about this girl and how she looks at me makes my world spin in another direction. She doesn't seem to care who I am, which has pulled me into her gravity. You always hear people talk about that moment when you meet the person you will spend the rest of your life with. Where in the hell did that thought come from? That never happens in real life. That's just something people watch in those sappy romance movies. Shaking my head, I focus on the beautiful woman before me.

"Hi, I'm Tinley. It's nice to meet you." She places her hand in mine.

I feel a tingle go up my spine from the contact. What the hell was that? Just as I'm about to ask her a question, Brad interrupts, heading toward the meet and greet. Still unable to take my eyes off her, I know I must look like a straight-up crazy person just standing here watching her. Tinley tells Grace she'll see her this afternoon, and a tall blonde guy comes over to speak with her. I think I might have caught his name as maybe Chase or Chance or something, and a strange jealous feeling comes over me. I just met this woman and spent all of two seconds with her it's not like I have some weird claim on her. He finally asks if she would like to walk around the pit area with him. Being polite, she nods and says she would love to.

Seeing him place his hand on her lower back, ready to walk away with Malibu Ken, my mouth word vomits all over the place.

"Tinley, would you like to come with us to keep Grace company? Sometimes race day can be boring while I meet fans and go to the drivers' meeting."

Good god, what the hell is going on? I don't invite women to tag along, let alone go to the drivers' meeting after my meet and greet. That's my quiet place (insert facepalm here). It is the one time during the whole race day that I get to myself, but now I've got not one but maybe two extra people coming with me. This has got to be an out-of-body experience right now. Maybe I'm still asleep, and this is just a fantasy—meeting the girl of my dreams, who I didn't even know I was looking for, and now I'm waiting for a purple elephant to come into view at any moment. But again, those blue eyes and mouth-watering curves have me waiting on edge for her answer.

Looking between Malibu Ken and myself, she says, "If you're sure I won't be in the way," in that sweet southern accent that makes my dick come to life.

Why the hell am I acting like a teenager who's just got his first taste? Turning away from me, she tells Chase she's so sorry but that she will see him as soon as the race begins, and they can talk some more. Yes, Ryan 1, Chase 0. *Take that, Malibu Ken.* Okay, I do know the guy's name, but to me, he's competition, and I always win.

"Okay, let's get this day going," Brad yells to the three of us. I can't help but glance at her every few steps and wonder if she felt the spark like I did when we touched. I notice a few other drivers looking at this gorgeous woman, and she has absolutely no idea that guys look at her, which is even more of a turn-on. Yep, I need to get this in check before the green flag drops. I want to pull her close to stake claim like a caveman so that the other drivers looking her way know that they don't have a chance in hell, but damn, who's saying I do? She seemed a little invested in Chase when they said goodbye. The way she touched his arm when they finished talking had my jealousy meter up a few notches. Glancing at her as she fiddles with her glasses.

"Tinley, tell me a little about yourself," I say, wanting to get as much information about this woman as possible during our little walk to the meet and greet because I knew we could be interrupted by someone wanting a picture or autograph on our walk at any moment. When she glances at me with those piercing blue eyes, I lose my train of thought.

Moving closer to her as we walk, my hand finds the small of her back, and I hear her breath catch just a little as she answers my questions. "Well, I'm originally from a small beach town in North Carolina." She shrugs. "I didn't want to move too far from home for college, so I decided on App State in Boone since I love the mountains but still wanted to be close enough to drive home if I needed my beach fix," she replies, rubbing her hands down her sides.

"I'm a mountain person myself. I love winter. Before falling in love with racing, I wanted to be in the NHL," I tell her. Shifting us away from the car coming down the alley, heading toward the garage. "What are you majoring in?"

"I'm an English major. I want to work for a publishing company after finishing school in a few months." I look down at the asphalt as we stop for me to sign an autograph.

"So, are you able to work anywhere you want?" I ask her, becoming very invested in what she has to say.

She brushes her hair out of her face, the sun already heating up the asphalt. "Yep, pretty much, which is great," she replies. "What made you want to be a race car driver?" she asks, looking up at me.

"I won my first bike race when I was about five years old. I thought hockey might be my career path when I got a little older, but racing just pulled me in and never let go."

She laughs at my answer. "So, you're just like every other

driver out here, then, huh?" she says with the cutest smile, playing with her glasses again, then looking up at me.

"Wow, don't hold back on my account," I can't help but say when she looks at me with those bright blue eyes. My mouth goes dry, thinking how I could get lost in those eyes. A tiny smile crosses her face, and the cutest dimple appears.

Walking into a meet and greet is always a fun time. Normally, we're surrounded by other team members and drivers. Sitting down next to my teammate and best friend Matt, he must notice the stupid smile on my face. "What the hell have you been up to this morning, McKenzie? You look like you have a clothes hanger stuck in your mouth."

Just as I'm about to tell him about Tinley, a little boy dressed in my number comes up to get the first autograph of the morning. That shuts down his questions before they can even begin.

"Hey little man, how are you?" I ask the little boy, who can't be more than five.

"Hi," he says shyly.

"Are you enjoying the race weekend so far?" I ask trying to make sure the little boy knows he doesn't have to shy around me.

Slowly he looks up to his dad before a big smile comes across his face. Finally, he opens up and begins to tell me all about his day, from checking out the cars to getting to meet other drivers. Laughing, I can't help but wish I had half his energy.

"McKenzie, quit hogging the little man. Maybe the rest of us would like to talk to him, too," Matt says before laughing.

"Well I hope you have a great rest of the day, and make sure not to root for this guy," I tell him, thumbing toward Matt, who is giving his famous smile.

After two hours of signing my name, taking pictures, and answering questions, I am beyond anxious to get out of there. Every now and then, I get to catch a glimpse of Tinley every so often and I get lost yet again in those curves of hers.

I can't complain too much because if it wasn't for my fans, I wouldn't have the life I love so much. I stand up, telling Matt to have a good race and enjoy coming in second to me. Making my way over to the dark-haired beauty I have become entranced with, I realize this race day is turning into one I won't forget.

Starting our walk to the next event, we continue with the questions. Tinley asking me questions now. "If you could pick one part of the race day you enjoy the most, what would it be? Honestly, I love the moment right before the race starts. That's when all the excitement comes crashing down, and I'm left with just the job I love. After signing a few autographs before heading into the drivers' meeting, I find myself glancing over at Tinley standing with Grace and Brad taking in the craziness of my life. A small part of me wonders if she might welcome the idea of going on a date with me or if I should just enjoy our time together now. I guess there's only one way to find out. I take a last look at her before ducking into the meeting.

Chapter 3
Tinley

The sound of the racetrack starts to become a relaxing sound, from the hustle of the crew member running from point A to point B to the loud engines coming from the garage area. I had been in awe of this man since we stepped out of the meet and greet. His sweet nature with the children making sure that he answered any question they had and playing along when the parents could tell the kid was a little shy to make them comfortable. As I stand back with Grace and Brad, my head spins a little, trying to figure out Ryan.

Grace has said Ryan was a big deal, but I didn't expect him to be so down to earth. I'm taken aback just a little. The man is gorgeous. But the way he carries himself strikes me as something different. I'd be lying if I said I haven't looked at him more than a few times since we got to the track earlier today. I snuck admiring glances at his tall, slender frame, light brown hair that's grown out just a little, and green eyes with little yellow flecks in them, with just the right amount of scruff that was so sexy. Every so often, I could feel his eyes on me and it made my skin prickle with awareness, and I found myself fiddling with my glasses more than normal. But Ryan makes me want to be more forward and brave with what I want.

Out of the corner of my eye, I notice a tall blonde standing off to Ryan's side, waiting for her turn to speak with him. I can't help but feel a little pain, wondering who this woman is and if she's just a fan or something else. The way that she's standing closer to him tells me that she may know him. But that's none of my business. I've just met this man, so why am I acting jealous?

As she goes in to hug him, I can't help but notice he seems to tense just a little. There's history there. Nudging Grace, I ask, "Do you know who that is talking with Ryan?"

Looking up, Grace finds the tall blonde, and the recognition on her face tells me she knows this person. That's Serena. She and Ryan were the 'it' couple a few months ago, but from what I've seen in the papers, they haven't been seen together in a while."

A pang of jealousy tugs at me, but I push it away. I have no claim to him. I don't even know him, for that matter. Shaking out of my fog, I start to walk again.

We head inside when Ryan finishes taking pictures and signing autographs with those waiting outside the divers meeting building. Brad follows Ryan toward the front of the room while Grace and I stay toward the back.

With NASCAR being a new sport to me—yes, I live under a rock, I know. Just because I live in North Carolina, the racing capital of the southeast, I'm told, doesn't mean everyone watches it— I pay close attention to what is being said about today's race and what is expected of all the drivers and crew members, so I'll have something to talk about with my friends and their boyfriends once the race starts later.

My mind drifts to Chase. He came along with James to be my spontaneous plus one. Finding Ryan's gaze on me sends butterflies fluttering in my stomach. I may never understand how I have not one but two gorgeous men wanting my attention on the same day, but as weird as it is, it makes me feel great about myself. I give myself a mental high five. With the drivers' meeting finally over, I tell Grace I'm going to meet up with everyone else and that I'll see her later. Giving her a hug goodbye, I head out to meet the others, looking forward to the beer that Miles promised me. This morning has me kind of off with the looks that I got as we walked around with Ryan, the extra attention is a little jarring, but also, I gotta say I enjoyed it. Plus, the guys are going to be jealous that I got to go to the driver's meeting because it was a big deal, and only certain people are allowed in.

As I head toward the stands to meet up with the group, I'm texting Mia to let her know I'm on the way. When rounding the corner and leaving the garage area, I slam into what feels like a brick wall. Stumbling back, a strong arm comes around my back. I brace myself for a fall that doesn't come, thanks to that pair of strong arms. Looking up, I see Ryan standing with me in his arms.

"I am so, so sorry, Ryan. I guess that's what I get for texting and walking. I can barely walk on flat land without falling." Laughing, I grip his ripped biceps, trying to get my feet under me.

He chuckles as I ramble on. "Well, I'm glad you slammed into me then and not some other driver," he says in a low, sexy voice. Is he flirting with me? Was he actually interested in what I had to say earlier?

"Thank you again for letting me tag along today. I'm sure Grace is really enjoying getting to see all this behind-the-scenes stuff."

Standing straight once again, I turn to walk away. Grabbing hold of my elbow to stop me in my tracks. I look up into those beautiful eyes; anyone would be lucky to get lost in. He asks the simplest question: "Tinley, let me take you to dinner."

I'm sure shock is all over my face. He gives me a smile that I can only assume works on all of humanity, making me blush. Tilting my head and crossing my arms so that he thinks I'm at least considering turning him down—I mean, come on, I wasn't, but I can make him sweat a little. Finally, I say, "Umm, why me?"

"Well, to be honest, you intrigue me. You don't seem to care who I am, what I do for a living, or even what I can bring to the table with my paycheck. I like that you call me out. If I might act cocky, I'm just intrigued. Give me one date. Let me show you I'm not a guy just looking for a girl on his arm or this famous driver who has a massive ego."

Has he ever had to work for a date? I wonder, laughing to myself, and when I look up, he's hanging on my answer, just waiting. "Okay, one date," I say, coming back from what felt like an out-of-body experience.

Curvy girls don't get the head turns like others, and I learned a long time ago that I'm okay with being in the background, but it's starting to feel nice to have eyes on me, and I'm embracing the attention more as the day has gone on. But this beautiful specimen of a man has really thrown me.

"Okay."

"Hand me your phone," he says.

I smile as we exchange numbers and wish him good luck on the track today.

Turning to walk away, he stops me again. Glancing up, I can tell he wants to say something else but instantly becomes nervous. Me – Tinley, the bookworm, made this famous NASCAR driver nervous.

"Did you need something else, Ryan?" I finally ask, standing by the haulers with my back resting against it. We stare at one another as crew members rush by, preparing for the race day.

"I just want to do one more thing before you leave, Tinley," he quietly says, bracing his hands on either side of me against the hauler.

Then he kisses me. It isn't just some friendly goodbye kiss— this is an earth-shattering never want to come back from heaven kiss that happens once in a lifetime. I feel my body heat as I press against him, instantly knowing he feels the same. If we don't stop, we're going to be on the front page of every tabloid magazine and internet article with this impromptu make-out session because it could turn even hotter quickly if I don't back away. Coming up for air, I look up at him with the biggest smile.

"Enjoy the race today, Tinley. I'll call you later about what time to pick you up for our date." He smirks.

With a final peck on the cheek, he turns and walks toward his hauler, leaving me standing there with butterflies in my stomach. Wow, talk about a turn of events. Things might just be starting to look up for ole Tinley.

Spinning around on my sparkly chucks, I make my way to the stands to find my friends. The track is loud, and as I get closer to my seat, people are dancing around, and beer cans already litter the stands. It's early in the day, but I can already tell that NASCAR is a party from the time you wake up. You either watch the race or pass out, but it's a fun environment. I can't help smiling, but I need to get it under control, or I will have to answer a million and one questions from my friends the moment I see them. Unless Grace has already texted the girls to tell them, which is very likely, she knows that some things are kept between us.

As I find my seat, my eyes connect with Chase's, and a smile comes to his face. He's sitting with our group, laughing and making jokes with the guys, and the girls seem to have embraced him too. A pang of guilt comes over me that I just kissed Ryan, yet here is Chase, excited to get to know me. But now that Ryan has come into my vision, I'm not sure that I can see myself falling for Chase. He may have landed himself in the friend zone before he even got a chance.

"Hey," Chase says. "Did you enjoy the tour? It must have been pretty interesting to get an up close and personal look at what happens behind the curtain."

"Yeah, it was neat, even if I have no clue what really happens at these things." I can't help but laugh.

"Honestly, it's easy to understand. I promise it's straightforward. If you have any questions, I'll be glad to help," Chase says with a smirk.

"Thanks. Hey, any chance the boys haven't drank all the beer yet? Miles promised me one, and I could use it. As you can tell, I'm out of my element."

"Of course, I made sure to save you a few, and I meant to tell you earlier you look beautiful."

Blushing a little, I can't help but stare into his eyes for a beat. How did I get myself into this position with two gorgeous men wanting my attention on the same day? Some girls would just say, "Hey, let's test drive both and see what happens," but I'm not that girl. The spark that I felt with Ryan is definitely something I want to explore and see if it actually is something. For once, I'm not going to sit back and be the quiet bookworm that everyone thinks I am. I'm going to grab life by the horns and have fun.

Chapter 4
Ryan

By the time I get back to my hauler, Brad and Grace meet me at the door. The minute I left the drivers' meeting, I was on a mission to chase her down. I knew I would be met with questions when I got back, but I'm not prepared for the look Grace is giving me right now. She looks at me as if I've just done bodily harm to someone, and she is ready to go into damage control mode.

"Ryan, explain yourself now," she says as soon as I step in the door.

"What are you talking about?" I ask.

As she stares at me, I think to myself, *Yep, she needs to be in PR. She could scare the devil himself straight with the look I'm getting. Brad better watch out, or she'll have his job. Matt could use a woman like this on his team because his PR guy sucks; I'm just saying.* With that thought, a small laugh comes from me, causing her to glare even more.

"Ryan, I saw you leave the driver meeting in a rush to catch up to Tinley," she finally says. "Listen, I know it's your personal life and all that shit, but she's my best friend, so it's my duty to tell you if you're just looking for a girl while you're in town, she's not it! She's the marrying type of girl, not the hook-up kind of girl, okay."

Grace is protecting her best friend, so I need to tell her this is different and make my intentions clear, even if I'm unsure of what I'm really feeling now.

"Okay, thanks for the warning, but just so you know, Tinley is different than any other woman I've come across, and I intend to see if we have something that could be more than just two people who hang out, if you really want to know. Now if you will excuse me, I need to get my head on straight to run 300 laps because this morning has taken a different path than my normal race days." *Instead of daydreaming about a curvy, dark-haired beauty taking up a lot of space in my mind.*

Stepping into the shower to get ready for the race, my mind wanders back to that kiss. I can't help but wonder if she also felt the earth crack. It may have been the most intense first kiss I have ever had. I would have kept kissing her for the rest of the night if I didn't have to prepare for the race. There's something different about Tinley. I want to get to know her and am determined to pull out all the stops to get what I want. The longer I think about her, the harder I get, water pelting me in the shower as I slowly start to stroke myself. Closing my eyes, I picture that dark-haired beauty kneeling before me with those blue eyes looking up so innocently before wrapping those beautiful lips around my cock. The image causes me to stroke fast, and then I'm coming all over the shower wall like a high school kid. Shit, what has this woman done to me?

Slowing my racing heart, it's time to suit up and go to work. Race days are always busy, so by the time I get buckled into my car, I'll be in a different headspace. Standing by my car listening to the national anthem, my mind keeps drifting to Tinley, having her standing beside me as I get ready to climb in, kissing me good luck and saying she will see me after the race. I've only known her for a few hours, and she is already occupying my mind. *Ugh, focus, McKenzie. You have a job to do and a race to win.* I need to get into driver mode, fierce NASCAR driver Ryan McKenzie who doesn't take any shit from anyone.

The rumble of the car's engine coming to life pushes Tinley to the back of my mind. I line up to begin 300 miles at Bristol,

The Last Great Coliseum. "Okay, Ryan, let's get ready to go green," I hear my crew say over the headset. "Bristol is a fast-paced track, and you need to be on your game."

The race is brutal from the start. Qualifying mid-pack, I knew I had my work cut out for me early on. The rookie doesn't make it any easier when he dives into the corner on lap 160, thinking he could pass me, but little does he know I'm not the easiest person to get around. After playing back and forth for ten laps, I've had enough and decided it's time to put him in the wall. Am I going to have a meeting in the NASCAR hauler? Maybe so. Time to head to the front. It will be challenging with only 50 laps left, but I'm up for it.

After 300 miles and a hell of a race, I end up with a top-5 finish. I always want to win, but the car just wasn't what it needed to be. Stepping out, Brad greets me along with the press, chomping at the bit to ask about the race today and about why I put the rookie in the wall. I put on a friendly face even though I'm unhappy with the finish. I need to be grateful for the life I'm able to lead by driving for a great team like Mac Motorsports. But really, I just want to get a shower and text Tinley to see if she enjoyed the race and find out when I'll be able to see her again.

As I'm getting my hanns device off, Regan Smith with Race Hub comes over to ask a few questions, bracing for the one that everyone's been asking. "So, Ryan, why did you put the rookie in the wall? He wasn't happy about that when he came out of the infield care center."

"Honestly, Regan, I was tired of playing his games. I had the better car, and when he wouldn't give an inch for me to get around him, I made my own inch. It's racing. Sometimes it happens; the rookie had better get used to it."

Two hours later, I finally leave the track. My mind races as I try to figure out what to say to Tinley. One kiss—that's all we had shared, and some light conversation. Yes, it was the best kiss I have ever had, and that makes me both excited and nervous as hell about what's to come next.

Pulling my phone from my pocket, I decide to text her. My first instinct is to call, but then I think that if she's riding home, she may not want to talk in front of all her friends, especially if Malibu Ken was sitting with her. What if they hit it off during the race? Did he ask her out? Did they hold hands? Had he made her laugh or even blush? I'm going down a rabbit hole of doubt, and I just need to text her to see if I even have a chance. *Deep breath McKenzie just freaking text her and see what happens.*

Sexy Driver:

Did you enjoy the race today?

Tinley:

Um, who is this?

Sexy Driver:

Sorry, yeah, you might need to know that - this is Ryan.

Tinley:

Ha-ha, I knew who this was just wanted to make you sweat a little. But your number is in my phone with Sexy Driver as the name. I wonder how that happened? Yeah actually had a lot of fun, and great job on the top-five finish.

Ryan:

So, what time can I pick you up?

Tinley:

Well, I should be home in about half an hour, so around 9 if you still want to do something tonight. I know you may be tired from the race, but if not, there's a bar around the corner from where I live. What time do you need to head back to Charlotte?

Ryan:

I'll see you a little before 9, and don't worry about me. I don't have to be back in Charlotte until bright and early Monday morning. So I have plenty of time.

You couldn't wipe the smile off my face at the thought of seeing Tinley later, what she might wear, and how the clothes would hang on her beautiful curvy body. *Good god, I've never thought of myself as the boyfriend type or even a romantic, but I'm starting to think I just might try for her.*

Grace's statement comes screaming to the front of my mind. *She's the marrying type, not the one-night-stand kind.* I know this date will be different. I have a lot to prove, not only that I can be what Tinley wants but that I deserve someone like her.

Chapter 5
Tinley

Between falling asleep on Chase's shoulder to texting a certain hot race car driver, my girlfriends were about to go crazy wanting to ask all kinds of questions. I was praying to god that they could wait until we got in the house before interrogating me.

When we arrive home, the girls push me out of the car and toward the door before I even know what's happening. Turning around to face them, I say, "Guys, I need to say goodbye to Chase. Y'all kind of just left him sitting in a car along with the rest of your men. I liked hanging out with him. Not sure if it's anything more than a friendship, but he's nice. And ladies, you might want to say goodbye to your men as well, considering they all look like a bunch of lost puppies. You all got out of the car like it was on fire."

Walking back over, I find Chase with his brow scrunched up, looking around in confusion, and James laughing as he gets an explanation out of Grace about what the hell just happened. Giggling at the scene before me, I wave for him to get out. "Chase, I just wanted to say I had a great time at the race and getting to know you."

"You're a remarkable woman, and I can honestly say I'm glad James asked me to come," Chase says.

I don't realize I'm staring at the ground until he places his finger under my chin and makes my eyes meet his. His kiss is gentle with a hint of more, and I'm so lost in the fill of his perfect lips that I forget we aren't alone and standing in the middle of my front yard.

A cough from behind us breaks the connection, and the blush I feel creeping up my face speaks volumes of the kiss I had just had. "I'll call you tomorrow, Tin," Chase says as he walks back toward Miles' Suburban.

When I turn around and walk toward the house, I feel like I hit the million-dollar jackpot. Not only did I step out of my comfort zone, I think I might actually like Ryan. The kiss with Chase was so sweet and safe, but I just didn't feel the spark.

Walking into the living room, the girls start with the questions I knew were coming. "You don't get to just basically make out on the front lawn and not expect us to have a million questions ready to come at you." Mia is the first to speak up.

I look over at Grace and realize she already knows what happened at the track, but she also saw my kiss with Chase a few moments ago. So being the bitch she is, she gives me a big smile and keeps right on like nothing happened, waiting for me to spill.

"Tin, it's been a while since I've seen that smile on your face, so what's up?" Lily finally says.

"Ugh, Ryan McKenzie asked me out to dinner. There, are you happy?" I say, falling into my favorite chair, the words coming out of my mouth before I even know what's happening.

The volume of squeals from my girlfriends is so loud I'm sure I go a little deaf at that moment. "Okay ladies, I need to get a shower and figure out what I'm going to wear. He'll be here at 9."

Looking at my best friends, I can't help but laugh. You can tell they have a million and one questions about what happened today and how I ended up having a date after kissing Chase in front of everyone. Lily finally asks the thing they all want to know. "Are you excited to go, Tin?"

"I am. He was sweet at the track and wanted to get to know

me as we walked to the meet and greet, then the drivers' meeting, which was nice." I blush a little, thinking about that world-tilting kiss. "Plus, ladies, he's a really good kisser."

Grace looks at me and laughs. "Yep, there it is. I knew you kissed him. He had far too goofy a smile on his face when he got back to the hauler, and he ran after you following the meeting."

I feel my cheeks getting redder by the moment. It makes me feel good, knowing he had enjoyed the kiss as much as I did. "Help me find something to wear. It's just casual, okay? We are going to the bar around the corner for drinks and dinner."

Following my longer-than-normal shower, making sure every inch of me is washed and hair free, just in case, I walk into my bedroom to find three different looks laid out for me. My best friends each have a particular style, and these outfits tell me who picked what.

Grace is the boldest, so I'm not surprised she wants me to be the 50s bombshell—\tight leather pants, a tank top with a jacket to go over it, and ankle boots.

Mia knows my style is simple, so she's laid out a pair of dark skinny jeans, an emerald green V-neck t-shirt, and my go-to pair of cream-colored Rothys I absolutely love to wear with everything.

Lily, the romantic of the bunch, picked out a pretty pale pink summer dress and my white chuck tailors to make it more me.

As I stand there wrapped in a towel, I wonder what tonight means to Ryan. Am I just another track girl? Or does he want to see me more than this weekend? I shake my head to get those thoughts out because tonight, I want to do one thing: just have fun and maybe continue what we started at the track.

Okay Tinley, time to get ready for a date with the most gorgeous man you may ever see, because God only knows if I will ever get this chance again. Finally coming back to the present, I decide to go with the green shirt, black pants, and boots. It's a casual outfit and one that I feel comfortable in.

At nine o'clock on the dot, the doorbell rings. "Ladies, I think I may throw up. Seriously, why the hell did I agree to do this? He is so far out of my normal. It's crazy, right? Yep, it's totally crazy," I yell to them as I round the corner from my room.

My friends look at me like I've just grown three heads. As soon as I stop rambling on, they start to laugh. Why the hell are they laughing at my freak-out right now?

"Tin, are you panicking because you may actually like Ryan?" Mia asks.

"Okay, I may be doing that, but guys, look at me. I'm not the "normal" trophy wife, or girlfriend material for that matter, you see on the arms of those drivers. I'm thick, a book nerd, and I don't run around in thousand-dollar shoes with perfect hair all the time. Most days, I'm in yoga pants, and my hair is in a bun on top of my head."

When I start pacing around the room, they finally step in to stop my spiral. "Tin, I'm going need you to come down off this ledge you're on right now and open that door because a guy is standing on the other side that genuinely seems to want to get to know the person you are." Grace finally snaps me out of my crazy rant.

With a deep breath, I open the door. Ryan stands in front of me, wearing the most beautiful smile any girl could ask for. Dark jeans hug his slender frame, and dammit if he doesn't have his hat on backwards. What is it about a guy and a backwards base-ball cap that makes a girl weak in the knees? At that moment, all my anxiety about tonight falls aside.

"Hi, Tinley," Ryan says to me.

"Hi," I reply. I feel myself blush just looking into his beautiful green eyes.

"You look beautiful, and these are for you." He hands me a beautiful flower arrangement.

"Thank you, you don't look half bad yourself," I say with a wink, which makes him smile even more.

"Are you ready to go?" he asks.

"Yep, let me just put these in some water," I say, before grabbing my purse as we head out the door.

As we walk toward his truck. I'm kind of surprised he drives a blacked-out Ford F250. I was picturing him as a top-down sports car kind of guy. So, it's great to see he doesn't take himself seriously and think he needs to be flashy. I feel my girlfriends staring at us. Turning around, we wave goodbye, just like I'm in high school out on my first date. Ryan meets me at the passenger side, opening my door for me. It surprises me a little because guys don't do that as much as they used to, and it is refreshing.

I thank him, and he says, "My mom would kill me if I didn't open the door for a lady."

"How very gentlemanly of you," I say, batting my eyelashes at him.

I buckle my seatbelt. As Ryan starts the truck, a song by Morgan Wallen, "Chasing You," comes on the radio. Smiling to myself, I can't help but think this could be a great night, and it makes me laugh just a little, which catches Ryan's attention.

"Care to share with the whole class what's so funny, Miss Cash?"

Looking over at him, I say, "I was just thinking we may have more in common than I thought. Well, at least your music taste isn't terrible. I love this song. I'm a fan of all kinds of music. Right now, I have New Country on repeat with my Spotify, but who knows? Tomorrow it may be 70s Rock or Elton John all day. At one point, I had The Greatest Showman soundtrack in my head for almost a week, so I'm kind of all over the place."

"I got to say I wouldn't have pegged you as an all-over-the-place kind of music girl if I was a guessing man, to be honest," he said.

"Yeah, I get that. My parents didn't leave the radio station on anything specific for longer than a verse, so I jump around a lot. What about you?" I ask, wanting to find out more about him as we head toward the bar. It's a short ride to the Twisted Pear around the corner.

"I love all kinds, but lately, I've been listening to a lot of New Country, Morgan Wallen and Luke Combs styles. But if you were to look at my Spotify List, you would find almost anything on my playlist also."

"Is there anything you listen to on race day that you normally don't at other times?" I ask.

"Huh." He taps his fingers on the steering wheel. "I guess I've never really thought about it, to be honest. It's just whatever I have on my playlist at the time, I don't have a race day playlist, but maybe I should," he replies with a laugh.

As we round the corner to the restaurant, I'm relieved to see it isn't crowded.

Just as I open the door to get out of the truck Ryan is there. Reaching for his hand a spark goes up my arm. OK , That is something I haven't felt before. Looking up to thank him, I can't help but wish he would kiss me again sooner rather than later. But hey, we'll start with dinner and see what happens.

Chapter 6
Ryan

Walking up to the Twisted Pear, I can't help but be relaxed talking with Tinley. She makes all my nerves go away with one look. If this is how a relationship is supposed to be, then go ahead and sign me up because I'm a goner for his woman.

There isn't a huge crowd—at nine o'clock on a Sunday, I would hope not—so I breathe a sigh of relief that I don't have to worry about us being bothered by race fans coming up to ask for autographs. I want to focus on the dark-haired beauty in front of me. Tinley makes her way to the hostess stand and requests a table. They're able to seat us right away.

As we walk toward the back of the restaurant, I place my hand on the small of her back. She looks up at me with the sweetest smile, and I want to kiss her in front of everyone to let them know she's mine. I shake my head at the thought.

"Your waitress will be right with you," the hostess says, snapping me out of my caveman thoughts. I thank her and ask Tinley if she has a preference about which side of the booth she sits on. "If you don't mind, I usually face the door in case a crazy person was to come in. My dad taught me a long time ago to always be alert when out in public. So I naturally take the seat facing the door," she says.

I can't help but chuckle a little at the notion of her protecting us. There's that caveman again.

"I'm fine to sit with my back to the door so that you can keep an eye out for us, but you do realize that I'm supposed to protect you, right?" I say with a wink.

"Maybe so, but also, it will keep all the eyes off you if you're not facing the door, and I know that you would keep me safe, even if we just met," she says, then adds, "Well, Ryan, tell me about your day."

"It was actually very eventful." I reach across the table for her hand. "I met a beautiful woman at the track. Had a decent run today, but it wasn't what it needed to be to win, but that's part of the game, and now I get to be out with said beautiful woman tonight. What about you, Tinley?"

"My day was different from any other I've had since moving here, that's for sure. My first NASCAR race, which I have to say, was a lot of fun. Going into it, I thought it would just be a lot of drunk race fans. Don't get me wrong, there were, but it was the most fun I have had in a long time. Met a nice guy in the garage area and got grilled by my girlfriends once we got home because of the smile on my face." A hint of pink tints her cheeks at the comment. "And now I am having dinner with said guy. I'd say I had a pretty good day, also."

It's so easy talking to Tinley during dinner, and I want to find out more about her. "What made you want to go into publishing?"

"Honestly, I love to read, and being able to take part in the process has always fascinated me."

"You had said your parents live on the coast. Do you get to see them much during the school year?"

"Not as much as I might like. We usually Facetime each other a few times a week. I'm close to them, so I miss them when I don't."

"Tell me about your traveling with the racing series. How in the world do you keep balance in my life with being gone almost nine months out of the year?"

"Honestly, it's not that hard. It's just me, so I don't have to worry about being late. Brad keeps me organized and just points me in the direction we are going next. I'm not sure what I would do without him by my side."

The conversation flows easily with Tinley.

When the server returns with our meal, seeing a woman that eats is so refreshing. Attending events with models, I've noticed they always go the liquid super route my ex Serena was always watching her weight and never wanted to go out to eat for fear of people watching her, which I always found odd, but it was her career to be in front of the camera. When the waitress comes back with my burger, I can't help but think, *Wow, this is the first time I've been on a date in a long ass time.*

"How's your burger, Ryan?" Tinley asks.

"It's really great. How's yours?"

"Really good. I love mushrooms on a burger. Some people think it's odd, but I've always loved them," she says.

"Well, I'm not a big mushroom person myself, but I've had them on a burger before, and it's not that odd," I say before taking a bite of my own bacon burger. I try hard not to groan out loud, but damn, this is a good burger. I should have known this place was going to have some great food. It's a dive bar in a college town. They always know how to cook.

After paying for the meal, we head out to the truck. I don't want the date to end. Talking with Tinley and just being around her has made me want her even more. Reaching for her hand as we walk toward the truck, I'm going to soak up every bit of the woman I can until I have to leave in the morning.

Chapter 1
Tinley

I can't help but think this was one of the best dates I've ever been on. Ryan wanted to know more about my passion for writing and my drive to go into the publishing world. It's a nice change from the ones I've been picking. As he opens the door for me, I can see he wants to ask a question but is unsure how to, so I finally say, "Do you mind if we make one stop before we go back home?"

He smiles. "Sure, what do you have in mind?"

"I want to show you my favorite spots on campus if you have time."

Driving toward school, I'm a little nervous. Normally, I save this spot for myself. For some reason, I feel pulled to show Ryan. I smile a little when we stop at the top of a parking deck.

"Umm, Tinley, are you planning on murdering me?" A small laugh comes from Ryan, and I can't help but laugh too.

"No, not yet, but I must warn you, I have watched enough FBI shows to have a good idea where and how to hide a body." I give him a wink. "Come on, big tough NASCAR guy. Get out. I want to show you something."

Getting out of the truck, I approach the far corner of the parking deck. This is my favorite place to come when I want to be alone, miss home, or have a bad day or a great day. You can see all of campus and clear to the blue ridge parkway, lit up like a huge Christmas tree. Maybe that's why I love it so much.

Christmas was my favorite time of the year growing up. Looking out over campus, I sense Ryan coming to stand behind me. When I turn around, those beautiful green eyes watch me. He reaches up, brushing my hair away from my face, and I know, in that moment, I slowly falling for this man, but also that I need to be very careful with my heart. It has only been a few hours since we met, but this isn't just a one-date kind of thing between us. He sets my body on fire with just the simplest touch, running his hand down my side and resting it on my hip. I can only imagine what sex would be like.

"Tinley, I've been wanting to kiss you since the moment you opened that door tonight," he says into my ear, making goose-bumps erupt all over my skin.

My cheeks heat at the thought of him wanting me all night. Gazing up into his eye, I ask, "Well, why haven't you?"

His lips are on mine before I finish my sentence. The kiss starts out tender, making my knees weak. Then it turns into an urgent all-consuming kind of kiss, like he's a dying man and I am the only thing keeping him alive. As he pushes past my teeth with his tongue, I know I'm a goner, and a small moan spurs the kiss on even more.

Pressing my body into his, I can feel just how much he wants me, and that turns me on even more, eliciting another moan from my lips. Knowing that this gorgeous man is turned on by me makes my core heat with such an awaking I didn't even realize I had inside me. I see pure lust as I break our kiss and stare up into his eyes.

I shake out of the lust bubble for a second. Ryan is going to have to put in the effort with me. He's not going to snap his fingers and have me on my knees. Granted, I so want to go there, especially with how he's looking at me, but I have to be strong for a little bit to see how this plays out. My mind races trying to imagine how beautiful he must look naked and how perfect his dick must be. I can already tell it's a little more than average but not so big it would scare the crap of a woman, and that's just from the friction during the mini-make-out session we had.

I take a step back from Ryan, catching my breath and thinking to myself, Good *god, woman, what the hell are you doing? This could be the dumbest thing on the face of the planet to not go full force at him. Because if the kiss was that amazing, the sex will be too.* But with the life he leads, I'm sure he has girls throwing themselves at him on a weekly basis, and I don't want to be in that group.

Ryan clears his throat slightly, adjusting himself. "Tinley, I've had a great time tonight. I'd really like to see you again. I've got to head back to Charlotte in the morning to get ready for next weekend's race. I'd love to call you this week, maybe Facetime also, if you're able to.

Looking up at him, I can't help but smile, "I would love that."

"Okay, great," he said.

We walk back to his truck, holding hands. The ride back to my house is quiet, with just the radio playing in the background.

Pulling into the driveway, I can't help feeling a little sad that I'm not sure when I might see him again. When I got home from the race earlier tonight, I decided to do a little research and see how much Ryan traveled during the season, and it's a lot. They kind of jump all over the US during the nine to ten months period. They even spend almost a whole month in Florida at the start of the season.

"Ryan, can I ask you a question?" I say, looking up at him. "How would this work? You're gone so much, and I'm finishing up school. I don't want to start something, then I only see you when you're in the state or over video chat."

"Honestly, Tinley, I don't know. I've never wanted a relation-ship. But I want to try with you. A lot of the guys have girlfriends and wives, so it's doable. And I would love to have you in my pit box when you are able to come. Just tell me you will think about it. I really had a great time getting to know you tonight, Tinley. Honestly, I think you're pretty great."

"I did, too, Ryan." As I sit there looking down at my lap, I can't help the doubts that come into my head. Could this be too good to be true? Could two people click like we have and work in the end?

He leans over, cupping my cheek and turning my head so I'm looking at him. Then he kisses me. Yet this kiss is different, sweet, and sexy at the same time, a longing or maybe a question of what if. I want to kiss him forever in that instant.

"Let me walk you to the door," he says.

Slowly we walk, and I become more anxious again. Part of it is because I'm trying to play out each option in my head on how it will work, and the other part of me is trying to keep my restraint and not dry hump him on the front porch for and everyone to see. I'm sure Mrs. Nelson doesn't need to see that.

"Thank you again for tonight and the race. Please thank Brad for letting us tag along with Grace. It was nice of him."

I turn to open the door but stop when it's pulled back closed. Turning to face Ryan, I'm met with his beautiful eyes, dark with lust again, and I am putty in his hands. I feel that heat rush into my cheeks once more.

"Tinley, I can't just let you go inside without a proper goodbye."

His perfect lips crash into mine, and my world stops spinning. And I know from now on, all other kisses will be compared to this one.

Chapter 8
Ryan

As Tinley reaches for the doorknob, I know in that instant that I can't let her leave without another kiss. What on earth is this woman doing to me? We've known each other for less than 24 hours, and I already can't get enough of her.

One kiss will never be enough, and I know it. The kiss on top of the parking deck was like you only read about. Having grown up with sisters, yes, I've read bits of their romance books, so I'm very aware of the spark and time standing still and all that shit, but never thought that I might experience it. We were so wound up from that kiss, and I wanted to do so much more. Let's just say that my dick didn't agree and was very unhappy about me putting the brakes on. But I knew she deserved better, and it sure as hell didn't need to be on a first date. She wasn't like the track girls that just wanted to have fun, say they slept with a driver for their Instagram followers, then go on about their night.

Pulling Tinley against me on her doorstep once more is such a natural reaction. Kissing her is like breathing; I have searched my whole life for this connection. She smells like lavender and honey, and with each kiss and moan, I know I have to get back here as soon as my schedule allows, or I'll make a point to bring her to me. Our foreheads press together as we catch our breaths once more.

Smiling up at me with those ice-blue eyes, she says goodnight. As I turn to walk away, I can't help but glance back at her, standing with her best friends on the doorstep with her fingers pressed against her lips. Throwing my arm up, I wave goodbye to the ladies, and I hear the laughter behind me as they pull Tinley into the house.

I sit in my truck for a few seconds, smiling at the night I just had with her. I also need a minute to get my dick under control because I'm hard as a rock, wishing Tinley was under me right now. Guess it's going to be a very cold shower when I get back to my hotel room.

Driving to Charlotte the following day is uneventful. With Boone about two hours from Charlotte I didn't need to leave extra early, but I wanted to be at the shop early to go over everything. Some weeks are better than others, depending on how we run. Mondays can be a mix of emotions. The garage guys could be unhappy with me if I happened to get into a wreck and the car is worse for wear.

Working for one of the larger race teams has some perks, like knowing my car is being set up and ready for the next weekend. I don't have to spend much time talking with the engineer to ensure the specs are right. So, I make my way down the hall toward my crew chief John's office. He's been my crew chief for a few years, and he is always easy to talk to if I have any issues, work-related or personal. John has been in NASCAR for as long as I can remember and knows all the ups and downs that come with the job.

"Well, well, look what the cat dragged in."

I walk into John's office. Looking over my shoulder, I notice Matt, my best friend and total pain in the ass teammate, sitting in the corner reading a magazine. We started in NASCAR around the same time, becoming fast friends. The media likes to call us Shake and Bake. Yep, from that terrible NASCAR movie a few years back. They could have given us something better, maybe from Days of Thunder. Matt McCall is the total opposite of me. Where I would rather wear vans and music t-shirts, he's a cowboy boot country boy from top to bottom. His blonde hair is grown out longer than usual, and he has a thick Alabama accent.

I walk further into John's office. The oversized desk, which he always makes a point of saying he hates because he's not a freaking CEO, is neat and organized with all the stats from the race weekend for us to go over.

"And just where have you been all night, Mr. McKenzie?" Matt asks with a smile so wide you can see his teeth from space. Flipping him off, I plop down in the seat beside him.

"I decided to stay at the track a little longer this weekend," I say, sipping my coffee. But I know Matt isn't buying anything I'm selling.

"Well, if that's the story you're sticking with, okay then." Matt laughs.

"Tell me why you're in here catching up with my crew chief, dipshit."

"No reason. Just wanted to see you do the walk of shame on a Monday."

Clearing his throat, John finally speaks up. "If you girls are done, I have actual work to do. If you want to know why Ryan didn't call you last night or stop by for Cosmos, then do that on your own time. Now give a goodbye kiss, and you'll see each other at home later."

"All right, I'm going. Ryan. beers later?"

"Yeah, I'll text when I'm done for the day."

An hour later, I finished my meeting with John. Considering the place we finished, it wasn't as terrible as I thought it might be. Granted, he wasn't happy about the fine I got for turning the rookie, but I'll do it again if the little shit gets in my way. John is just as competitive as me, so we're always extra hard on each other come Monday mornings race breakdown. Just as I turn toward the engine shop, I get Brad's text wanting to see me. I let out a loud sigh because I made sure to be on my best behavior this weekend—well, besides the little bit of damage control he had to do with me turning the rookie, but other than that, I was good since we had an extra guest in the pit box this weekend. *What have I done now? I better go find out before checking on my car.*

Taking an abrupt turnaround from the shop, I head over to the management side of the building to see what I've done.

Walking into Brad's office five minutes later, I find him at his desk studying his iPad. Well shit. This can't be good. His face looks like he's ready to explode.

"Hey Brad, you wanted to see me?"

"Hey yeah, come on in. I wanted to check in and make you aware of some things that have come across my desk this morning."

Turning his iPad around, my jaw falls open. In front of me is a picture of myself and Tinley at the track, sharing our first kiss.

"Brad, who did you get this from?" My blood starts to boil, and I know I need to get my temper in check, and quick. But the more I stare at the picture, the worse it gets. Then I notice the hateful comments about this beautiful woman.

Some comments range from, "What could that gorgeous man see in that girl? She's not a model. She likes food too much," to, "I bet she only wants him for his money," to one that says, "Another pit lizard for Ryan McKenzie."

"Brad, you better be doing something to take this shit down. That's what I pay you for!"

"Ryan, of course I'm doing everything I can, but it's not just one picture. There are a few. Did you stay in town last night to go on a date with her?" Brad asks.

"Why does it matter if I did?" I rub my palms across my jeans to get my anger under control.

"Ryan, if you are going to date someone, that's fine with me. Hell, I had a front-row seat to the instant connection when I saw you at the race with her. I can tell it's something different. But, if you really like her, you need to prepare her for this life. Your career comes with photographers, fans, the good and the bad, and sometimes the occasional enemies. She needs to be all in, or you have got to let her go. You cannot string her along; just know that."

Sitting back in my seat, I can't believe I've gone through every feeling possible in less than two days. I run my hand through my hair. I need a beer or five. So, I decide to text the one person who will talk me off this ledge and figure out what I need to do and say to this amazing woman I can't imagine not having in my life.

Ryan:

Hey, I'm gonna need you to come over for that beer extra early.

Matt:

Sounds serious. I'll be over in 15

Ryan:

Yeah, thank I need some advice only you can give me.

Grabbing the beer out of the back of my truck, I hear the rumble of my best friend's loud-ass dodge charger. You could hear that redneck thing from space if the wind blew just right. Matt jumps out, smiling without a care in the world. Rubbing my hand down my face, I realize this feeling right here is why we stay single. Not having to worry about the shit storm or consider another person's feelings or the media having a field day with it.

"Well, I'm here," Matt yells. "what's this big emergency that has us day drinking like college frat boys?"

Walking into my condo, this was the first big purchase I made when signing with Mac. It's three bedrooms, but the huge kitchen sold me. Granted, I don't even cook, but it's great for when my family visits and mom makes her amazing fried chicken. Well, that and the view overlooking the lake.

"Come on, I need advice only your smug face can give." With a smile and shrug, Matt follows me inside the condo. Sitting on the couch, beer in hand, I try to figure out how to explain my weekend with Tinley. Then I get up and pace the floor.

"Um, bud, your kind of freaking me out right now. Did you get someone pregnant, or do I need to get a shovel and help you bury the body? I just need to know which best friend speech to get together for you, man," Matt stated.

"Yeah, I'm kind of freaking myself out, too. Okay, here goes. I met a girl."

"Okay, that really doesn't tell me what the problem is," Matt says. "We meet girls all the time, have some fun, have them sign an NDA, and go about our day. I'm kind of confused about why this is a big deal."

"No, Matt. It's not that kind of girl. Her name is Tinley, and honestly, she's amazing. She came to the track this past weekend with a friend who Brad was helping with PR work. The moment I set eyes on her, she got into my head and set up camp. That's why I was late coming back from the track this weekend. I made a trip to Boone to take her out on an actual date and see if there may be something there."

"Wait, was that that curvy dark-haired girl with the smoking hot blonde at the meet and greet?" he asks.

"Yes, it was. Now, will you help me, please?"

"Wow, never in my days did I think you might actually find a girl that you would say was worthy of your time," Matt says with a laugh.

"Matt," I say, rubbing my hand down my face, "I need your help figuring out if I want to expose this sweet, sexy girl next door to the sometimes-crazy world of NASCAR. She had never been to a race until last weekend and had no idea who I was. In the back of my mind, I think that attracted me to her more because I could just be Ryan with her."

Sitting back on the couch, beer in hand, my best friend just stares at me. What the actual hell is happening right now? My mind is racing as fast as I drive, and I don't know which end is up. It's like I'm in an end-over-end roll, just waiting to hit the ground.

"Matt, you've got to help me with this. When I went to check on my car, Brad called me into his office to show me pictures of us kissing at the track. It's all over the internet, so I know she's going to see them, and some of the comments are terrible. I need to know how to handle this without hurting her." Scrolling through my phone, I pull up a few pictures and show them to Matt.

Finally joining in on my mental breakdown, Matt says, "Hold up. You met a girl over the weekend, went on a date, and now are freaking out about a picture? Wow, this girl did a number on you in a matter of two days. I think I need to know two things, okay? First, why would you care about some pictures? They follow us around all the time. Did you not see them when you were out? Second, does she have a friend for me? That blonde was smoking and that body… damn."

I punch him hard in the shoulder. I can't help but laugh at the craziness that has become my life, but hell, Tinley makes me feel something I can't explain.

"Ouch, Okay," Matt says after laughing at me like I'm a crazy person for overthinking this with Tinley.

"I'm assuming after this weekend, you want to see if she may fit into our world, correct?" he asks.

"Yes, Matt. That's why I've got you over here in the middle of the day, acting like a twelve-year-old girl with a crush. It's just that she's not like the track lizards that come and go. I haven't done a serious relationship since I started in the series. I really don't want the media to have a field day with her, she doesn't have a model frame that I am normally seen with, which I absolutely love, but you've seen the comments, and I don't want it to hurt her."

"Well, the way I see it, you have two options. You either go all in or bow out now. But from the way you talk about this woman already shows me the direction you're going. You just need to hit the gas," Matt says. Statements like that are why he's been my best friend for as long as I can remember. He knows exactly the way my head works, even when I have no clue.

"And by the way, you never," he throws his hands above his head dramatically, "answered my question about whether her friend is single, and you can hook up, your best friend." And there he is, my pain in the ass, making a stressful situation light again.

Laughing at his gesture, I can only say, "Um, I'm not sure on that front, but let me get my legs under me. Then maybe we can find you a nice quiet girl as well."

"Hell man, I don't want a quiet one. I want the woman who will leave marks on my back and call me Daddy," he says, laughing.

Standing up from the couch, I look over my shoulder at Matt and say, "I think I'm going to head back to the shop and talk with Brad. Maybe he's got a handle on this, and I won't even have to worry about it. Or I'm going to have to come back here with my tail between my legs and have you help me send a text message. Because as of right now, you have been no help except for the laughing at your buddy department."

"I'll be here when you get back then, bud. I'll have dinner ready when you come back with your tail between your legs," he says, laughing.

I grab my keys and head back to talk with Brad. This is turning into one of the longest freaking days of my life.

Chapter 9
Tinley

S itting in my Monday morning lecture is about as fun as a
root canal. I hate math. That's why I put off this final math
credit. How the hell people did this every day boggled my mind.
As I sit in class, I get the feeling that people are staring at me. I
hate being the center of attention, much less the talk of the town.
When I look up for the third time during my hour-and-a-half
lecture, I see Chase staring straight back at me. How in the hell
had I not noticed him in my class before? I feel my cheeks heat
from the attention as the professor finishes the lecture and gives
the assignment for the next class.

"Hi, Tinley," his deep southern voice says. Looking up, I can't
help but notice he is so very handsome, and our brief kiss comes
to mind after the race. Yet when I meet his eyes, all I can think of
is Ryan.

"Would you like to grab a cup of coffee? Chase asks.

*Okay, Chase is a great guy, but why haven't I seen him in my class
before? Have I been so focused on finishing this school year that I blocked all
men from my mind and eyesight?*

"I'd love to," I say.

"Okay great, lead the way." Chase gives me a sweet smile as
we head toward the campus coffee shop.

"Chase, I honestly didn't know that you were in my math
class."

A small laugh comes from his lips, and I can't help but feel a few butterflies when it happens.

"Tinley, I have a confession. I'm not taking that class," he says as we continue heading toward the coffee shop. "I just wanted to see you again, but I didn't know if I even stood a chance after your date with Ryan McKenzie."

I stop in my tracks and stare into his beautiful, sweet, and concerned eyes. "Chase, how did you know I had a date with Ryan?"

"Umm, I'm guessing you haven't been on social media lately, have you?" Pulling his phone out of his pocket, he shows me the pictures making the rounds. Photos of Ryan and me, some at the race and others on our date. Grabbing his phone, I stare at the images, my hand shaking and a wave of nausea coming over me. Passing him the phone back, I shake my head.

"Chase, I am so sorry, but I'm going to take a rain check on the coffee. I need to go talk with Grace and figure out what the hell is going on."

"I understand, Tinley. Would it be okay if I got your number? Honestly, I would really like to get to know you better. I kind of thought we might have something between us at the racetrack the other day, and the kiss was one I haven't forgotten."

"I'd like that, Chase."

We exchange numbers, and I head off on my mission to find Grace and tackle my next issue. One I didn't even know I had until about ten minutes ago.

I make a point to not be on social media. I don't have a personal Instagram page, just my Bookstagram, which I love, but it is different. My book connections are some of the best I could ever ask for, and they always check in with how school is and what guys I met. But I haven't even filled them in on the weekend.

Picking up my phone, I text Grace:

Tin:

Hey, are you at the house?

Grace:

Yep, just walked in the door. What's up?

Tin:

I was going to have coffee with Chase
when he asked me about my date with
Ryan. I need your PR skills.

Grace:

I'm on it

Tin:

Great, see you in a little.

That's one of the great things about Grace; cool under pressure and would go to hell and back if needed for her friends. But if you ever cross her, you better look out because that Grace is fierce.

When I get to the house, I feel the start of a headache. As I walked from campus, I could feel everyone watching me, and I was already over being the center of attention. Making my way over to Grace sitting at the table, laptop open, I know the answers to the questions I want to ask. I've had them since the moment I kissed Ryan. I really like him, but I don't fit into his world.

"Grace, tell me, I don't need any bullshit right now," I said.

"All right, well, you may not like this, but as your best friend, it's my duty to tell you." That makes me recoil just a tad. "Tin, there are pictures of you and Ryan on your date this past weekend and your kiss at the track. Someone caught that one, also. Some of the comments are not nice at all." As Grace continues talking, I grab the laptop, bracing myself for the onslaught of hate. I saw the photos when Chase pulled them up but didn't scroll to the comments. I was too caught off guard to look any further. The vultures commented on everything from my weight to my clothes and my favorite one, "Why did he choose a girl like her?"

"Have you talked to Ryan today? It's still early, so he may not have gotten to the garage yet." Grace says.

Looking down at my phone, I think about how we had a great time yesterday & last night. He told me he enjoyed it, but here we are, almost lunchtime, and not a single text. I know he's back in Charlotte. I can only bet Brad showed him the same pictures Chase and now Grace have shown me by now. Then why hasn't he texted me to see if I'm okay? That little doubt comes in. Even though he said I was special, am I just a weekend girl? I need to get some answers. The Internet trolls don't bother me, hell I've spent my whole life with this body, and I know I can't change that, but what hits harder is that Ryan didn't even text. He lives with the media every day, yet it's a completely foreign thing for me, so it makes me wonder, does he not think I'm worth it?

Grace gives me a few options. Since I don't care to have any social media accounts, those won't help. "Well, first, you need to call him. Hell, I might even say go to Charlotte and demand some answers. I can call Brad and see if he's dealing with this, which, if he knows me well enough, he's expecting my call anytime," Grace says.

"Okay then. Let's go."

I'm a woman on a mission; I need answers, and I'd rather get them directly from him. It's not like I'm ready to burn the town down mad—I'm more confused, but the least he could do is talk to me about it. If he's going to hide and vanish like a ghost, I'm going to hunt him down like a freaking ghostbuster and get to the bottom of it myself.

Chapter 10
Ryan

As I pull into Mac Motorsports for the second time today, I honestly still don't know what to say or if I can even put a sentence together that might not make me seem like a dick. Which, now, I one hundred percent feel like. I still haven't checked in with Tinley, and I know the longer I put it off, the worse it's going to be.

Walking up to Brad's office, I notice the door is closed, which is a little odd because I just called Brad to let him know I was on the way. He said he was free the rest of the day and that I could come on down.

I knock on the door and hear Brad say, "It's open."

What I'm not expecting is to be met by a beautiful pair of ice-blue eyes. It isn't only Tinley but a very angry Grace. Remember how she could scare the devil straight? Well, that's the face I'm getting.

"Brad, what's going on?" I tear my eyes away from the very frosty glares I'm getting from Grace.

"Ryan, let me tell you what's going on," Grace says.

Her anger is justified, and I expected it. Her best friend is all over the internet just because I wanted to spend time with her. Then I couldn't even be the stand-up guy and call her. Yep, I'm officially the asshole in this story now.

"Tinley went to class today, only to find out that her entire life has now been posted online. She didn't hear it from you like she should have if you were a decent human being. Luckily, Chase was the one to see her and make sure she was okay," Grace finally calms down and explains.

Great, Malibu Ken beat me to the punch to make sure Tinley was okay because I was in my own head and didn't even send a fucking text. Now here she is, sitting in Brad's office, trying to figure things out.

In that moment, my head and heart come together, and the groveling kicks in. "Tinley, I am beyond sorry for the pictures that got out of our kiss. And the position that I've put you in. It never even crossed my mind that we would have people follow us because I honestly enjoyed the time, I spent with you. I should have been more cautious and looked out for you. I am sorry the track pictures are on the internet for all the world to see, but I wouldn't change that first kiss for anything. And when you think of it, it's kind of cute. I mean, how many people can say they have evidence of their first kiss?" I try to make a joke, but looking at her face, I know it didn't hit where I wanted it to. "I should've checked in, gave you a heads-up. I just hoped Brad and I could run interference first or have more progress before I did."

"Ryan, I'm going to need you to stop talking," Tinley chimed in. "I had an amazing time on our date. The pictures honestly don't bother me. What I have a problem with in this whole thing is that you didn't call or even text me. Just something simple 'Hey Tin, I had a nice weekend, and by the way, there are pictures on the internet of our weekend.' As soon as Chase showed them to me just before eleven o'clock, I knew in my heart that Brad had already shown you the same thing earlier in the morning since you told me that you usually came into the shop early on Monday mornings. So you would have met with him about something like it wouldn't have gone unnoticed by him if he's doing his job. Yet here we are, almost eight hours later, and not a single word. Why couldn't you even send me a text!"

Standing like a block of wood, letting Tinley's words register,

I suddenly realize I do not want to have this conversation with an audience.

"Brad, Grace, can you guys give us a moment in private to talk?"

Closing the door behind them, I let out a long breath. I knew this day would be long, but hell I didn't think it would turn out like this.

"Okay, before I do or say anything else stupid, let me first start by saying I am so sorry for the invasion of your privacy today. I've been trying to figure out what to say since the moment Brad showed me the post this morning." I come around the chairs to sit beside Tinley. "I promise I'm not avoiding you or blowing you off like I can only assume you think. I'm also guessing that you believe this weekend was just nothing. Tinley, I can assure you that is so far from the truth."

I inch closer to her. I feel her breath catch, and I know she feels the same thing as I do, and I'm not about to let whatever we had over the weekend end just because of pictures on the internet.

"Again, I am so sorry. You must understand that I would never do anything that would hurt you. I really like you and want to see where this can go if you'll still have me. I know Chase is also interested in you, but I would really like to try." Laying all my cards out on the line and keeping my heart open, I wait for a response.

"Ryan, I know you didn't expect this to spiral the way it did, but the issue is how you went about it and not talking to me. If we are going to be together, you must communicate with me. I had no idea the media watches you as much as they do. NASCAR is new to me, and I just think of you as a guy who I like and had a great date with. I don't see you as this superstar. So, if you really going to be with me, then I will have to come to terms with the fact that this is a part of it."

Why was this woman so perfect? Here I am, feeling like a

complete ass for not talking with her sooner, and she's trying to make me feel better.

As she stands up, I think she is getting ready to leave the office, but she surprises me.

Coming to stand in front of me, she straddles my lap. All I can do is stare up at her and think, *how in the hell did I get so lucky that this sexy woman wants to take a chance on me?* I may have fucked it up just a little with our pictures getting out, but I'm damn sure not going to let that happen again. I would protect her with my life.

She wraps her arms around my neck, so naturally, I graze her ear and feel her shiver a little, kissing the side of her neck. I knew that she was going to be responsive. Even after our short time on top of the parking deck, I'm already starting to read her body. Leaning closer, I pick up my pace, kissing along her neck.

"Tinley, tell me to stop."

The slow humming coming from her is all I need to keep going. As I kiss her, running my hand over her breast, pulling on her hardening peaks. I know she's enjoying this as much as I am. "What if someone comes back in here?" she finally asks breathlessly.

"Tinley, I will worship you in private or in front of an audience if you just give me a chance. Kissing her hard and with the passion she deserves, I run my hand over her heat ever so slowly, I'm already hard as steel, and it wouldn't take more than a few pumps, coming all over myself. Unbuttoning the top of her shorts, I look into those blue eyes that hold my attention and live in my dreams, waiting for her to tell me to stop, but that doesn't happen.

I run my hand past her panty line. She's slick for me already. Playing with her clit has her moaning so loud I'm sure the shop guys can hear her. Pinching the sensitive bud brings another beautiful noise from her mouth, and I try to smother it with a rough kiss.

"You like that, don't you, kitten? It turns you on knowing that someone could walk in here and see you riding my hand like a good girl."

"Yes Ryan, please."

I insert one digit into her tight pussy and thrust my hips up, seeking my on-rush. Just as I pull my finger out, she protests, but I'm so turned on it just spurs me on even more. I thrust two fingers into her amazing pussy again, this time a little rougher. With my thumb circling her clit she rides my hand just the way she wants.

"Ryan, yes. Keep that up. I'm going to come."

"Kitten, use me like I know you've thought about since the other night."

If the way she is grinding up against me as we kiss is any indication, she knows it and is trying to torture me as she gets closer to her release. Just as I reach the point of no return, I feel her clench around my fingers, and the most beautiful reaction comes across her face, one that I hope I get to see for the rest of my life. Pulling my hand away, I lick my fingers clean and watch as her pupils dilate. I think to myself, *Yes, take it in, kitten, because I'm about to ruin you for any other man.*

Tinley has branded my soul and possibly my heart in this moment, and I will never be able to let go. For once in my life, racing isn't the center of my world. Tinley is becoming my driving force. Will we both be willing to risk it all for love? Or will we crash and burn trying? Either way, I'm damn sure going to find out.

"Tinley, I know one thing for sure I want to get to know you better." I eye her up and down in the most obvious way possible. Seeing her cheeks heat with desire, I kiss her again, just the way she deserves. Pulling her closer, wanting this beautiful woman to know I'm not just looking for a weekend adventure. I'm looking for the weekdays, too.

As our mouths meet again, a small moan comes from her lips,

and I know the answer to my question before she even has a chance to tell me. The longer she straddles me, rubbing against my already hard dick, the more I want to make her come again, but the next time will be with me inside her. I pull back slowly, knowing if I don't stop myself, I will have my way with her on top of my PR agent's desk, and I don't think he would like that too much.

"Okay," she says quietly, her cheeks still flush from our make-out session and the orgasm I just gave her. I can't help but smile so big with just that simple statement. This beautiful sexy woman is giving me a chance, and I'm going to make damn sure I don't mess it up.

"Would you like to come back to my place? I'll gladly drive you home later if Grace wants to head back to school. If that's okay with you."

"I'd really like that, Ryan. I still have a lot of questions about all this, and some privacy might be nice. Also, I want to continue what we started here," she says, kissing my neck as she stands to make herself presentable before leaving Brad's office.

Chapter 11
Tinley

Driving to Charlotte earlier this afternoon, I had this big idea in my head about how the conversation would go with Ryan. But now, sitting in Brad's office at Mac Motorsports after one of the strongest orgasms of my life and the little dry hump session, plan A has gone completely out the window. I know in the back of my mind we have a lot to figure out; a kiss and orgasm definitely won't change that. Yet my lady bits have a different take on the subject, and for once in my life, I will let them win this one. I have always played it safe, and dammit, I'm tired of being that girl. I'm ready to drive headfirst into this adventure and see what happens. Sometimes, the nice quiet girl is overrated, and I need to start embracing this other side that Ryan seems to bring out in me. Even if a small part in the back of my mind is just hoping my heart doesn't take the fall too fast.

"Take me home, driver," I whisper in his ear as I head for the door.

"I can arrange that, kitten," he growls, his eyes flashing with lust.

The more he calls me kitten, the more I'm starting to like it. That may be because of all the romance books I've read, but I've always wanted to be called a sexy name by the man I was with.

Grabbing my hand, he jets past Grace as we leave Brad's office, not giving her a second look, only shouting, "I'll have her home before classes tomorrow." I briefly look over my shoulder and see Grace gesture the call me sign before rounding the corner headed toward the parking lot that Ryan's truck is in.

I have never been so turned on in all my life. Ryan isn't like any of the guys I've met before. I'm not the girl who gets swept off her feet, nor am I the girl being worshipped at all the parties or when we are out at the bar having drinks on the weekend, but damn, I'm glad I'm getting the chance to find out how it feels to be that girl. Score one for the curvy ladies out there.

"Where are we going, Ryan?"

"Well, from the please fuck me eyes you've been giving me, I'm taking you to my place. I planned to take you to dinner, be romantic, and do some more groveling because, honestly, I still need to do that, but now the only thing I want to eat is you, and I plan on doing that all night long," he says, his voice so sexy it sends goosebumps along my skin.

"Then you need to use those racecar skills, or I may just give you a preview in this truck in front of anyone passing us on the road," I say very sweetly. *Goodness, where did that come from?* Usually, I'm a soft-spoken girl, but Ryan makes me want to try new things.

I can't help but smirk when I hear a growl from him at the idea of another man or woman looking at me as we drive to his apartment. I want to be this fierce Amazon who knows what she wants and makes sure she gets it.

"Tin, I need to make a quick call," Ryan says.

He hits the dial button, and I see Matt's name come up on the screen.

"Hey, man," Matt answers.

"Hey, Matt. Are you still at my place?" Ryan asks.

"Yeah, remember you told me to hang out, and you would be back after you figured out your shit? So I'm here, waiting and drinking all your beer," Matt says.

I can't help but giggle at the conversation playing out between them.

With Ryan distracted while talking to Matt, a wild streak comes over me. Reaching over the middle console, Ryan sucks in a breath as he notices my movement and as he replies to Matt.

"I'm going to need your ass gone. I'm on my way back, and let's just say I've got plans that don't include you," he says.

My hand rubs his already hard length while he talks to Matt. A hisses come through his teeth, and his hips shoot up, pressing himself harder into my hand, wanting to see how far I can push him before he ends the phone call with Matt. Rubbing my hand over his length reaching for his zipper. It doesn't take much before he lightly moans, then remembers Matt is on the phone.

"Damn, dude. Didn't think I was going to get an X-rated call. I do, however, expect a call at some point. Hi Tinley, I'm glad you didn't kick his ass to the curb. He's kind of got it bad." Matt laughs. "And Tinley, if you happen to have a single friend help a guy out."

A chuckle escapes my lips. "Hi Matt, I'll see what I can do, I might have someone, but she's fierce. She's not a quiet church girl."

"Thanks, man. Now get the hell out of my house," Ryan says.

Ryan's rough voice echoes through me, sending a shiver down my spine. Although it's a demand for Matt to leave, it's also a promise of what is coming.

He hangs up the phone. When he speaks, his voice is deep and filled with lust. "Tin, I can promise you that if you start something in this truck, I will have to punish you as soon as I take this seatbelt off."

I shiver as his hot green gaze meets mine, full of a deep-seated need for whatever kind of punishment he might provide. I have never thought of being dominated before, but Ryan's threat sends an electric spark through me, making me crave whatever he might dish out. I'm already so wet for him; I'm sure my thong is fixing to fall right off. I push my luck just a little bit further.

Cupping his sizeable erection, I rub him faster to see how far I can take this little game on our ride.

When we pull into his apartment complex, I jump out of the truck only to be met with Ryan's large hand coming up around my neck and pinning me to the passenger door. "No, no Tin, what did I say about you teasing me all the way to the house?" Ryan says with a sexy smirk.

Swallowing down my nerves, my answer is both a confirmation and a dare. "That I would be punished." A deep blush crosses my face. I know he sees how he's affected me, and I want to be punished. Punished by him. As he holds me in place, I push my breasts up against him, needing the contact.

"Come on, sex kitten, I've got plans for you," Ryan says. I follow him, wanting the pleasure and the possible pain that this god of a man is offering.

Chapter 12
Ryan

T he drive back was interesting. Tinley had me wound so tight I needed a release and quick. Stepping into my apartment, I'm happy that Matt listened and is nowhere in sight. When I pull Tinley inside, I can't help but love the sight of her in my personal space. It doesn't feel weird. I don't bring women here. I like to separate my private life from my public; having her here means something. I've only ever had one other woman here, Serena, and looking back now, she wasn't what I wanted. She was just a means to an end, and we were both using one another when our schedules fit.

Closing the door behind me, I pin her against my chest. I notice her pupils dilating, and her breathing picks up. I need to taste this woman and brand her as mine so she knows she belongs to me.

"So, tell me, Tinley, what kind of punishment would you like? Or should I play out one of the many dirty thoughts that have been going in my head from the moment I set eyes on you at the racetrack?" I ask, grabbing her hair and forcing her to look up at me.

Slowly kissing down her neck while cupping her breasts and squeezing them roughly, I can't help but smirk when a moan comes from her perfect mouth. She's already so wet for me, I can smell her beautiful scent from where I'm standing, and I haven't even started. "Tinley, you have far too many clothes on for my liking, so we need to fix that now!"

With a giggle, she raises her arms. Removing her shirt, I'm met with the most perfect breasts I have ever seen. I kiss each one slowly, savoring them as I unhook her bra. Her nipples pebble, and her breathing becomes faster. My dick strains against the zipper of my jeans, and I'm about to lose all control if I don't get her under me.

"All right, sex kitten, I'm about to come like a teenager if we don't move from this doorway. Or I'm going to have my way with you up against it. My neighbors will hear you scream my name, but maybe that should be your punishment for the little stunt you pulled in the truck."

Another beautiful giggle comes from her lips. "Show me where your bedroom is, race car driver. I'm ready for that ride," she says.

"Good god, woman. What are you doing to me?" I kiss her hard one last time, then pick her up. Her legs instantly wrap around my waist as I return to the bedroom. "Ryan, put me down. I'm too heavy for you to carry to your bedroom," she says.

Stopping in my tracks, I look down at her, kissing her hard. "You are in no way heavy, kitten, and if I want to throw you over my shoulder in the middle of Victory Lane, you will let me. Your mine. Let's get that out of the way right now.

Throwing her onto the bed, I can't help but admire this beautiful woman laid out for me. The image is one I'll always remember, her dark hair laid across my sheets. The tiny lace underwear.

Seeing her cover herself up, a growl comes from my lips. "STOP!" I say a little more aggressively than I normally would. This woman makes me a caveman so easily. "You will not hide from me, gorgeous. If I have to tie those wrists above your head so you can be on full display for me, I will. Your body is what real men want." Slowly, I make my way down her body. I feel her tense up.

"Tinley, don't you dare be ashamed of this beautiful body. I plan to savor each and every part. But since you've driven me crazy getting here, I can't promise I'll be gentle, but I can tell you I'll make it up to you a few times over," I say with a smirk.

The most beautiful blush comes to her face as I strip her lace panties. Crawling back up her body, I kiss her so aggressively, it has me hard as steel. My head spins a little with anticipation, wanting to ensure she enjoys herself as much as I am. It's a weird thought. I always made sure the woman came, but I also didn't give extra attention to every part of the woman's body. I knew sex with random track lizards was no strings attached; a means to an end. With Tinley, I couldn't care less if I get myself off, but I'm damn sure going to make sure that she comes over and over tonight.

As I pull away, a groan in protest comes from her beautiful plump lips. Tracing my hand over her hip, I stop my descent, cupping her needy pussy, and a small whimper comes over her this time. Smirking, I ask, "Is my girl that needy for me to touch her?"

"Ryan, I may burst into flames if you don't touch me," Tinley states.

"Well then, I'd better make good on that punishment I promised you." I plunge one finger into her hot wet pussy, making her arch on the bed, her beautiful breasts ready for me to devour them. Making my way slowly down to her gorgeous pussy, glistening and ready, I bite down on her clit, nearly making her come off the bed. Sucking and pumping in and out of her, the sweet taste of arousal coats my tongue, making me work her over even faster.

With her moans louder, I pull myself away and can't help but smirk at the protest that comes from Tinley. Crawling back up her body, I hover over her mouth. "Would you like to taste just how turned on you are, kitten?"

"Yes, Ryan," she says in a needy voice.

"Ah, you're a dirty girl, aren't you?" Plunging my tongue into her mouth, I make the same motions with my finger while I kiss her. When I pull hard on her nipple, she moans. So my sweet innocent bookworm likes it a little rough. I'll have to remember that for another time. Pumping into her, her moans increase, and I take her other breast into my mouth, not wanting to miss one ounce of this woman's body. Inserting a second digit into her hot pussy, she becomes even wetter in my hand. "Tinley, are you going to come on my fingers?" I ask, wanting to hear her say the words.

"Oh god, yes, Ryan. Yes, I'm so close," she says. Bending my middle finger to just the perfect spot, I see the moment she lets go feeling her come on my fingers. As she relaxes, I pull out, and with her watching me, I lick my fingers clean. "Ryan, that was so hot," Tinley states, watching me suck her juices.

Reaching over to my nightstand, I pull out a few condoms because I know I will be fucking her more than once tonight. As I tear the condom open with my teeth, Tinley crawls over and strokes my cock. Her soft hands feel great on my already hard length. Groaning, I let her continue at her pace until I can't take it anymore and go to grab her hand, only to be stopped by Tinley shaking her head. "What do you want, Tin?" I ask.

"Well, you gave me not one but two amazing orgasms so far. Now it's my turn. So lay back. I promise when I get done, you can fuck me five ways to Sunday, but I want this beautiful cock of yours in my mouth first."

"Yes ma'am," I state, sitting back on the bed and watching this beautiful woman settle between my legs, so eager to make me come.

"Should I lick you like a lolly pop and make you suffer just a little before I take you as deep as I can, or just make you blow your load now?" she asks with a wicked grin.

"Tinley, I think if you just touch those beautiful lips to me, I'm going to come so hard down your throat, you will taste me for days. Suck me," he growls.

Doing as she's told; Tinley takes me in her mouth as far as she can before slowly moving up and down. My hands dig into the sheets trying to think of anything but this woman on her knees in front of me so that I can last longer than a high schooler getting his first blow job. Good lord, this woman knows what she's doing. My head is spinning, and just when I think she's going to let up, she cups my balls, sending me over the edge.

"Oh fuck, Tinley, I'm coming. Shiiiiiiiit." Letting out a moan, I relax and look down just as Tinley lets my cock go with a pop. Damn, that was the hottest blow job I've ever received. Jumping up, I kiss her so hard I can still taste myself. Pinning her to the bed, our kiss becomes hot and messy, and before I know it, my cock is ready to go.

"Are you still wet for me, Tinley?" I ask, already knowing the answer but wanting her to say it.

"Yes Ryan, please fuck me now!" she cries. I begin slowly unrolling the condom I laid beside me, but Tinley stops me. "Ryan, let me."

She grabs the condom, putting it on my hard length. I know she's doing it to torture me, and it's working. Grasping her hands, I help her finish, then push her back onto the bed, holding her wrist with one hand. I stroke myself a few times, then rub my cock over her clit, teasing her and making her squirm. Just when I think she's had enough and she's so wet, I thrust into her so hard that she cries out my name. Fuck yes, this is where I'm meant to be. Hearing her cry out my name makes me pick up my pace and pound into her hard.

"Are you going to be my good girl and take it rough, Tin?"

"Yes Ryan, harder, oh god, yes," she says. This woman may just be perfect, soft and sweet, but a dirty girl in bed.

Chapter 13
Tinley

To say that Ryan knows how to make a woman's body sing would be a major understatement. This man had me begging for more when I was coming down from the best orgasm of my life.

Snuggling into his arms, I can't help but feel content. And scared out of my mind. How is this ever going to work? We are from two different worlds. I'm quiet and reserved in my everyday life, and he's literally a rockstar of the NASCAR world.

"Tin, I can hear your mind working overtime right now," Ryan says as he cuddles closer to me.

"I'm sorry, I'm just trying to process how this could work, honestly. Why would you want me when you could have anyone on the planet? And believe me, I Googled you—

because apparently, I'm a masochistic. And let me tell you boy, was that a fun afternoon looking at those pictures—and your list is impressive with models and actresses."

"Well, would you like me to tell you why again? Because I will," he states. "Tinley, I'm not sure you give yourself enough credit, honestly. One," he kisses me, "you're smoking hot. I've had to jack more than normal since we met, and that's only been a few days . You have invaded my mind something fierce. Two," he kisses me again, "I like that you have your own opinion and want to have a career that could take you anywhere in the world. Three," another kiss, "you intrigue me. That's hard to find in my world when people are looking for an angle or just want to be with me so they can say they slept with a driver." Then he kisses me senseless, taking all my worries along with it.

Shortly after sleep overtakes me, I wake up in his bed and lay staring at him, sleeping like a stage five clinger. Deciding I can't lay in this bed anymore, I get up and throw a blanket over my naked body, heading toward the kitchen, hoping that a glass of water may settle my spinning thoughts so I can rest a little before heading back to school. That's the problem. I've been so insecure with myself for so long and have finally accepted who I am. I worry that being with Ryan and seeing pictures of us together could throw all those thoughts front and center again. Looking around his beautiful home, I'm stopped in front of his wall of trophies when I feel hands snake around my middle. "Hey beautiful, what are you doing out here and not in my bed?" Ryan asks in his low, husky voice.

Falling back into his arms, I state, "Couldn't sleep, so I came to get a drink of water and got distracted by all the trophies." I motion to the wall. "Tell me, which of these is your favorite?"

Laughing, he says, "That's like asking me to pick my favorite child, but if I had to, I would say The Brickyard 400. It's one of the year's best races, and winning that one sets you apart from other drivers." Spinning around to face him, I find myself lost in his beautiful eyes. "Come back to bed, Tin. We only have a few more hours before I have to take you back to school, and I don't want to miss a second."

"I can think of a few things I want to do with you before I go." I smile a sweet smile just as the blanket falls from my body.

"Well, Miss Cash, what did you have in mind?" he asks.

Dropping to my knees, I look up at this beautiful man, smiling as I take his throbbing dick into my mouth, loving the moans and grunts that come from him. "Pull my hair if you want, Ryan. I want you to use me. I'm not a delicate little flower like you may think. Or have you not already noticed that." If I only have this one night with him, before I have to go back to reality then I'm going to be bad and act out of character for once. Sucking a man off is not normally my go-to, but with Ryan, I want to. Knowing it will drive him wild, I sway my hips, getting into a comfortable position to take his dick in my mouth.

"You like that, Tinley? You like when I talk dirty and I fuck your mouth?" he asks.

He hits the back of my throat with his cock, and I can tell how much he is enjoying this and that he wants this just as much. The man loves to be in control, and he unleashes the second I tell him to use me. Tears run down my cheeks, and my moans grow louder. Ryan knows what game he is playing, getting me so on edge that I won't be able to control myself if he doesn't finish soon.

"Play with yourself, Tin, but don't you dare come. You do, then I will punish you. I can smell your arousal from here. I'm going to come all over those perfect tits of yours. I want you ready for me," he says.

Running my hand between my legs, I barely touch myself and nearly come just from the slight contact. Groaning from needing a release, I insert two fingers into my pussy and pump ever so slowly because if I pick up even a small amount, I will come.

"Shit Tin, you are so good at this, fuck yes." Ryan moans.

Pulling his beautiful cock from my mouth, he pumps it two more times and comes all over my breasts, with me staring up at him. Then he does the hottest thing I have ever seen, running his fingers through his cum and coating my lips as if to mark me as his.

"Stand up, Tinley," Ryan commands.

Rising to my feet, I can barely stand upright. Ryan walks us to the oversized chair in the corner of the room and sits down with me standing in front of him naked and so turned on that if I don't get off soon, I will combust.

I look down and see he is already hard again and wants me. "Do you have a condom in here?' I ask. And like magic, he grabs one off the table in the middle of the room. "Do you just keep them in each room for all your lady friends when they come over?" I ask, wondering if I want to know that answer.

"Nope, just when a certain curvy brunette is around." He smirks and smacks me on the ass before putting the condom on. "Tinley, RIDE ME!"

I straddle his lap, loving that he is both sweet and aggressive with me. He doesn't care that I'm not stick-thin. In fact, I think he likes my curves.

"So tell me, Ryan, would you like me to go slow?" I ask as I take his cock until I'm full and then pull back out. "Or would you like for me to go fast?" I slam down on his cock, making both of us moan loud enough to wake the dead. Gosh, I hope his walls are soundproof, or we may get a noise complaint after this one.

"Tin, use me however you want," he says, placing his hands behind his head, watching me as I pick up the speed, playing with my breasts as I find my pace.

Just from our little time together, I'm already picking up on things Ryan likes. He's definitely a fan of my breasts being a little larger than the average woman's. Have mercy on me. This man is going to ruin me for all other men. Watching him stare at me is so erotic as I ride him more, and my movements get faster; I'm getting so close to my release.

"You turn me on so much, Tinley."

I slam my mouth on his, and he takes what he wants. As he twists my nipple, I let out an even louder moan, and he pushes up with his pelvis, hitting the spot that drives me crazy and sending me right over the edge. "Oh God, Oh God, Ryan, yes, yes, yes."

"Yeah baby, you like that, don't you? You like it when I take charge and make sure you come harder than anyone has ever made you come."

"Yes, Ryan. Yes."

Spinning me onto the couch, he rails into me a few more times, keeping my orgasm going until he cries my name, finding his release. Sitting on this couch, he kisses both of my breasts as I come down from the orgasm and stare at him for a few moments. I could do this with him; we could. The media may not like me, but who cares? If this man will take a chance and wants me, then heart be damned, I will try.

"Yes," I say.

Ryan looks up at me. Laughing at my statement, he says, "Yes?"

"Right, you might need some context on that."

Ryan laughs again. "Honestly, I just thought you were saying, 'Yes, that was the best I've ever had, and you, Ryan, will never get rid of me. I'm ruined for all other men.'"

There's that smirk that I'm getting all too familiar with and loving. "Well, honestly, I thought that, but I was also saying yes to giving this a try. I can't promise that I will be easy to be with, and I have a ton of questions, but we can try a relationship if that's something you can see yourself doing."

He jumps off the couch naked as the day he was born, like he won a major race, a smile crossing his face at this simple word. Yes, three letters, but it's a step I wasn't so sure of twenty-four hours ago. He kisses me with everything he has. I'm a little light-headed by the time we separate, and I can't think of a better feeling.

Chapter 14
Ryan

I have never been a relationship guy. With racing, I never had time. Or if I had the time, I just choose not to have them. The second that Tinley said yes, I couldn't stop the smile from crossing my face.

Driving her back to school this morning, I already miss her, and she's sitting right beside me. Reaching across the console, I can't keep my hands off her. I want her with me all the time. Wow, am I sounding like a love-struck puppy, or what?

"Tinley, I want you to come to my race next week," I say. I look over at her, and she's staring at her lap and picking at her nail. "Tinley?" I try to get her to look at me.

"I'm so sorry," she finally says, "what were you asking?"

"I said I'd like you to come to my race next week. It's at Martinsville, which isn't a terrible drive to make from your school."

"Okay, yeah, I can do that. Would it be okay if I brought Grace with me? She's still trying to figure out her next move with her degree, and I know she would love the exposure if that wouldn't be too much trouble."

"Of course, that's fine with me. Bring anyone you like as long as I get to see you. That's all that matters to me. Just let me know a final count by Thursday so I can tell them how many passes I'll need to get."

Pulling up to her house, that feeling of loss comes at me

again. This may be the longest week of my life before I'm able to touch and kiss her again. Yet it will also give us the space to make sure that this is something Tinley can handle, with the racing schedule the way it is. It may be a few weeks or even a month before I can have her in my arms. I don't want to start this out with her under the impression that my life is a normal boyfriend. I guess that's why I don't bring women into my world. It will take a special person to understand the amount of travel I do ten months out of the year.

Stepping out of the truck, I notice Tinley hasn't moved. I open the door for her and help her out. I can't help but lean down and kiss her tenderly. This woman is like a flame, and I'm a moth drawn to it whenever she's near. Deepening our kiss, I wrap my hand around the back of her neck, tilting her as she moans so slightly that my tongue explores her so softly. When I pull away, she looks so beautiful with her large blue eyes shining up at me.

"Come on, sweet girl, let's get you inside before I have your legs wrapped around me in your driveway."

"Okay, that might be a good idea. I don't think my neighbors would like that kind of show quite this early," she says, smacking my ass as we walk toward the door.

"Honey, I'm home," she says, stepping into the living room just as Grace comes around the corner with a cup of coffee in her hand.

"Well, if it isn't Tinley Cash, doing the walk of shame bright and early and giving the neighbors a little show in the driveway, might I add," Grace says with a smug smile. I laugh at how open this pair is and hear Tinley groan beside me. "Well, on that note, I guess I better be going." Pulling Tinley into my arms, I kiss her again like a man who needs her as his next breath, and I could not care less that Grace is still in the room watching us.

"I'll see you this weekend, kitten," I say. Kissing her one last time, I head back to my truck. I feel I've left a little piece of my heart with the curvy woman taking up every waking minute of my brain. I never would have thought a woman would have so much power over me. Growing up, I was told when you find the right person, things will fall into place just as they are supposed to. The question is, is it her? Time will tell.

Tinley

"NEVER IN MY life have I wanted to be a fly on the wall more than I did yesterday in that office," Grace says as I turn around and walk toward my bathroom to get ready for my morning class.

Turning the shower on, I think about the last twenty-four hours—how his kisses made me want more, how his hands knew just how to play with my body. Running my hands over my lips, I still feel his kiss. Lost in my thoughts, I don't even hear Grace follow me into my room. Turning around, I scream when I see her watching me.

"Spill now! Tinley," she demands.

"Sorry, what? I can't hear you. I've got to get in the shower." Laughing, I jump in the shower, only to hear the seat on the toilet shut and Grace huff out a laugh.

"You know I'm your best friend, and I need details so you get to tell me while you're taking a shower because I'm not going anywhere," Grace states.

"Okay, fine. Honestly, it was amazing. I'm not just saying that because it's been a long damn time since I've had an orgasm that wasn't of my doing. He made me feel like I've always wanted. He didn't care that I wasn't stick-thin; he worshiped me, and let's just say, multiple times and in multiple spots around his place," I tell her.

"Well, from what I could hear outside the door, it sounded like he was very persuasive before you left Brad's office. You better lock that down then," Grace says with a laugh.

"Don't worry. I did last night. We are going to try to give this relationship a go and see what happens. He's got a lot of traveling coming up with the racing schedule, so we will see where I fit in his world. You're going to Martinsville with me this weekend, just so you know. That way, you can be a part of that world for your future job, and I can get some time with my man. So, make sure you have no plans and tell that man of yours you're busy."

Grace jumps up from where she's sitting and pulls the curtain from the shower. "Are you serious? That's amazing. Don't worry about the boy situation. I'm an independent woman, foremost. Thanks, Tin."

And just like that, my day starts off great. I spend the rest of the morning with a smile on my face, and nothing can change that, not even yet another boring math class I have later in the day. Ryan McKenzie found his way into my heart, and time will tell if this was going to turn into a fairytale or just an epic one-time love story I can tell my grandkids—*Hey, want to hear about when your Gigi went out with a famous race car driver before meeting your Pops?*

Chapter 15
Tinley

The week had been a whirlwind from school, catching Ryan on the phone when he wasn't busy getting his car ready for the weekend to trying to keep up with my girlfriends. I feel like I'm burning the candle at both ends, but I can see the end in sight. I only have two months of school left before graduation, so the clock is ticking.

Arriving at Martinsville, I'm both excited and nervous. Getting our passes and heading to Ryan's hauler, a wave of emotions comes over me, and as if Grace senses it, she grabs my hand, giving me a silent, "Relax, it's going to be fine."

Walking up to the massive rig, Brad meets us at the door just as he is coming out. "Hey Tinley, Ryan's just getting ready. Go on inside. I know he's been waiting to see you before the race."

"Thanks, Brad."

Stepping into the hauler, I see Matt sitting on the couch, scrolling his phone. "Tinley," he says, jumping up to give me a hug, "it's great to finally meet you in person." Letting out a small whistle, I see him look over my shoulder to Grace. Laughing a little, I step out of the way. "And who is this angel with you?" he asks, making his way to Grace.

"Yeah, bud, I'm going to stop you right there cowboy, I promise you can't handle all this ," Grace says.

Laughing at the interaction between our two best friends, I

head toward the back to find my man. "Hey, driver," I say before wrapping my arms around his midsection.

"Hey kitten, I missed you. Are you ready for your first race by my side?" he asks.

"Yeah, I guess, but honestly, I'm nervous and just want to make sure that I don't do anything dumb that's going to end up in the paper."

Trying to play it cool when Ryan asks me to stay with him during the pre-race, but my insides are freaking out with all the attention. I seem to wince at each flash or camera click, but Ryan reassures me each time and holds my hand as we walk from place to place. Grace, however, is in her element, soaking up each minute. Other than her having some back-and-forth banter with Matt, that's turning into something hilarious as the day goes on. But there's also there's something that I can't put my finger on— and that's one nut I'm going to crack soon because she does not want to talk about him. I think she seems to enjoy the day.

I ask so many questions during the race that I think the crew may be getting sick of me, but I finally understand how stages and points work. So. There are four stages in each race most of the time. Some only have three depending on the number of laps, and they can get points in each one to help with a run for the championship.

By the end of the day, I'm dreading leaving Ryan. I loved having his attention directed at me, and watching him on the track was such a rush. That suit he wore had me hot. Who knew something so simple would turn me on? But by the time midnight rolls around, I know we need to head back to school, even with the race being on a Saturday. Saying goodbye will be the one part of this relationship I'm going to hate. Kissing Ryan is starting to be one of my favorite things.

"Tinley, come to Vegas next week. I know you're busy finishing up school, but it's one of my favorite towns. I'll fly you out. You can stay a day or two with me, and we can have some us time while I'm not at the track."

Looking into those green eyes, keeping my heart and head in check is getting harder. "Can I let you know in a few days? I need to make sure that I've got my schoolwork done for the week."

"Sure, of course," he says. And with one last kiss, I head to meet Grace outside the hauler so we can make the drive back to school.

The following weekend, I'm on a plane headed to Las Vegas. Never in my life did I think I would be here, that I would be a driver's girlfriend. Am I his girlfriend? We haven't said those words yet or put a label on what we are doing. I wouldn't have gotten onto a plane and flown to Las Vegas to watch him if I didn't think it was going in that direction, right?

I sit up in bed. Ryan booked us in a room at the Paris hotel, a few miles away from the track in the heart of Las Vegas, just so that we are able to have time to ourselves. Scanning the room service menu, deciding on fruit and yogurt just so that I have something on my stomach because my nerves are getting to me this morning. Being the first time I'll be alone at the track I need to get used to it if this is the life I'm going to have with Ryan. Jumping in the shower while waiting for breakfast to arrive. I should finish getting dressed and then head to the track to see Ryan.

I text Ryan, letting him know that I'm headed to the track with him and leaving early this morning because, apparently, he has a routine on race day, and with me along for the weekend, it also included him giving me orgasms. And let me tell you, that was one hell of a way to wake up. Rounding the corner to the garage, I see Ryan standing beside his crew chief, John, talking animatedly.

John smiles and says, "Hello, Tinley, enjoying Vegas?"

"Well, from what I've seen, it's great. I'm not a gambler, so I'm okay to miss that part."

Grabbing my hand, Ryan brings it to his lips for a quick kiss. "Hi kitten, did you sleep well?" he asks with a twinkle in his eye because we both know we slept little. When I finally did fall asleep, he woke me again, but I'm not complaining.

"I slept great, Mr. McKenzie, thank you," I say, winking at him. "So, what's the plan for today?"

Brad comes around the corner with two coffees. "Good morning, Tinley. Here, I picked up a coffee. Thought you might want it," he says.

"Wow, thank you so much. It's like you read my mind. I was just asking Ryan what his schedule looked like and where I needed to go."

"Well, we have a meet and greet today, and that's it before the driver's meeting, so it's a slower-paced day for once." He laughs.

"Okay great, then I think I'll head back to the hauler to get some final items checked off for school, then meet you later, if that's okay."

"You sure, kitten? You can hang around here as I get things completed with my car," Ryan says.

"No, I'll let you do your workday process so your head is where it needs to be. I'll see you a little later." I kiss Ryan and head back toward the hauler to work just a little.

I can't believe this is my life lately, but I'm getting so used to it and falling more for Ryan the longer we spend time together.

STANDING BESIDE RYAN'S CAR, holding his hand as the national anthem plays, I can't help but notice those watching him and then looking at me yet again. I wonder what they think of us, how the women look at me, wondering how this curvy woman ended up with this gorgeous man. Yes, I've had these thoughts since we started seeing each other, but keeping them at bay when you're at the track is hard.

"Tinley, baby, did you hear me?" Ryan's voice pulls me from my thoughts.

"What? I'm so sorry. I got caught up in the hugeness of this moment." I blush slightly.

"Well, I said, give me a kiss so I can get to work." With a wink, he pulls me close, and all the surrounding noise disappears as he kisses me. Granted, he keeps it PG, but I can tell we both want so much more.

"Have a great race, my driver, and I have one more thing for you. I've been watching a lot of old races over the last two weeks, and I wanted you to have good luck from me while you race." I hand him a penny I had found on heads on my first day of college. "It always brings me luck, and it was in my pocket the day I met you. I'll see you after the race. Stay safe for me." And with one more small kiss, I walk toward pit row to watch the man I'm falling so hard for go to work.

Turning around one more time, I see Ryan strap into his car and focus on the race.

OKAY, whoever said racing was a fun sport has never had someone they were falling for as the driver going over 200 mph. My nerves are shot, and I have zero polish on my nails as we reach the race's final stage. That's one of the many things I have learned today from Ryan's crew chief. I think I bothered him more than I should have, but when John said that I could ask him anything, I don't think he thought that through as much as he could have because I have bugged the holy hell out of him. Granted, I got all my minor questions answered last week at Martinsville. I tried to get more in depth with car setup and how they can tell when they need to change car details and handling.

So far, my man has fared well with running in the top fifteen all day.

With headphones on, I've been able to listen to Ryan and his crew chief all afternoon, and it's been amazing to see and hear how in sync they are. And with just the little information he gives, they adjust the car. He gets better and better at each pit stop. With less than thirty laps to go, I hear his voice change. It sends a little zap of excitement into my body with how gravelly it becomes. He's come through the pack of cars with ease this last stage, sitting in third. John tells him how much fuel he's got until empty, which to me seems like a lot, but with the speed they are traveling, it could be a small amount. Let's be honest; on a good day, my car has the gas light on because I think I have more than I do.

A stern voice over the headphones says, "It's go-time. Stop playing around and win this damn thing."

As I look up from the monitor I've been watching, I see Ryan come out of turn four and dart to the outside of the car in front of him. Rising in my chair, I hold my breath as I watch him pass the second-place car with ease. He's a man on a mission to catch the first-place car. Fifteen laps to go. I'm testing my deodorant's strength at this level of stress watching laps tick down. I notice the crew members' pace and excitement take over. My man might win this race, and I'm here for it with him.

Just as they cross the start-finish line with three laps to go, I see Ryan go to the inside of the first-place car. I can tell that this driver will not be as easy to pass and may have to work for it. "Ryan, you're going to have a be more aggressive with Kevin. He's not just going to roll over. Even if we have the better car. He wants the win and the points," his crew chief John says over the headset.

"I'm on it. I just need to get him right where I want him," Ryan says.

As they pass the flag stand, they get the two-to-go signal, and Ryan tries again, this time on the outside. That line has been the best for him today, and passing that way has been easier. It takes every breath out of me watching him; he does it with such ease and courage to go at this speed each week. Coming out of turn four, I see Ryan's car in first and jump to my feet. White flag, that's it. One more lap, and I can kiss my man and tell him how proud I am of him. He eases into turn one, then two taking the backstretch two more turns. Holding my breath, I watch as he crosses the checkered flag.

I jump up, getting a little misty-eyed at how amazing he is. "Come on, Tinley, let's go see Ryan. When he gets out of the car, I know he will want you to be the first thing he sees," John says to me.

We make our way to victory lane in a cyclone of excitement. Watching from the sidelines, it's a dance of some sort—from the trophy placement to the crew knowing where to stand for pictures. I hear Ryan's car before I see it standing over to the side so they can have their moment with the crew when Ryan rolls into the winner's circle. Watching him get out of his car covered in sweat and smiling from ear to ear may be one of the sexiest things ever.

Jumping into his crew's awaiting arms to celebrate, they place him back on the ground, then I see him search for me. And that, ladies and gentlemen, is the moment that I fall in love. Yep, love, not lust anymore, but love. Like that great question on One Tree Hill, "Who do you want standing beside you when all your dreams come true?"

It's him!

Chapter 16
Ryan

WOW! We won and I'm exhausted. The last fifteen laps were a bitch to get under me. And knowing that Kevin was going to race me rough made it hard to keep my cool. We both needed this win to get the points to keep us in the championship battle. But when I saw him bobble going into turn three, I saw my chance and gunned it, leaving him behind me.

Rolling into victory lane, there was only one person I wanted, her, the curvy brunette that stole my heart and never looked back. Was it fast? Hell, I'm sure it was. Did I care that it scared the shit out of me? Nope, not even a little. Tinley Cash was my future, and I was making sure of that today.

Searching victory lane, I see her standing over by the side, tears in her eyes. I know she can't see me, so I sit in the car for a second and take in her appearance as she watches everything happening. What does she think of all this, and is she ready for this crazy ride with me? Taking off my helmet and hanns device, I exit the car as the confetti starts and jump into my crew's arms, our go-to celebration since I started with this group. We have become close since the beginning, and they are my second family. When they place me on the ground, I seek that dark-haired beauty I can't wait to kiss.

She's still standing in the same spot I saw her in when I pulled the car into victory lane. Walking over, I notice she's not paying attention to me but looking at the confetti raining down.

Reaching into the pocket of my fire suit, I fish out the penny she gave me before the race. "I think I have something that belongs to you, kitten," I say, getting her attention. Tears in her beautiful blue eyes take my breath away, and I don't say another word. I kiss her. I don't care that people are calling my name, taking my picture, or what the media may say tomorrow. My heart stops as I kiss her. This is the moment that I have waited for and did not even know it.

"Ryan," she says, breaking our kiss. When I look back, she's smiling so wide that I can't help but beam back at her with an even bigger one. "You won!"

"Yep, seems I did, kitten. Now come on and have your picture with me so I can say this is my favorite trophy I've won because this is the day that I fell for the most amazing girl, even more than I thought I could."

Grabbing her hand, we make our way to the crew, and they all circle around her like she has been a part of the team all along. "Tinley, are you ready for the hat dance?" John asks.

"The hat what?" She laughs as the first sponsor's hat lands on her head.

An hour later, we head back to the hauler. I would love to say I'm exhausted, but that isn't the case. I have so much adrenaline that I'd take Tinley right here at the side of my hauler if I knew we wouldn't get caught. Pulling her to me, I push her against the side of the hauler. I can't keep my lips off her any longer. I need her. "God Tin, do you know how turned on I have been since I saw you in victory lane?" I ask.

Giggling, she says, "I have a pretty good idea because I have been so wet for you since I saw your hot ass get out of that car."

I growl, "Get your hot self in that hauler right now and wait for me. I'll be there in just a second. I just need to check on Matt, that wreck he was in didn't look good, so I want to make sure he's okay and not drinking himself into a coma."

Pulling my phone from my pocket, I hit my best friend's

number. "Hello?" Matt says, sounding more out of breath than he should.

"Hey man, um, did I interrupt something?" I laugh at the way he answered.

"Fuck, what do you want?" he grumbles like I really am interrupting him.

"Just checking on you after that hit. I wanted to make sure you are okay, although it sounds like you are just fine."

"Yeah, I'm good. Look, I gotta go. We can talk on the flight back tomorrow. I umm, I gotta go."

"Okay man, but we will have this conversation about whatever is going on right now because this is just odd right now."

"Gotcha, bye." He hangs up before I even have time to say bye.

Well, that's one for another day. Right now, I have a girl that needs my attention more. Marching up the steps to my hauler, locking it behind me, and closing the front blinds for the night, I find the best sight I could ask for after a race. A curvy brunette with amazing blue eyes, naked in my bed.

"Miss Cash looks like you can follow directions when asked. Or are you just wanting my cock that badly?"

"Well, you asked me to. I thought I might be a good girl and do as I'm told for once."

Pulling her to the end of my bed, I kiss her how I've wanted to all day. Long and slow. Moaning, she says, "Ryan, please fuck me. I've been so turned on watching you I may melt if you don't right now."

"Well then, let me make sure you don't." I pull a condom from the bedside table. I only give her a second to watch before I thrust into her so hard she moves up the bed. "Is this what you want, kitten? Want me to fuck you hard and fast so that you can get off?" I ask.

"Yes, yes," she chants.

Coming close to her ear, I say, "Well then, hold on because

that's just what you're getting. But when I'm done, we are doing it my way next."

Kissing her neck, I flip her over and rail into her from behind. She's so turned on that it only takes a few thrusts, and she's coming undone and crying out my name. Slowing my pace, drawing her orgasm out, I make her shiver even more, then pull out.

"Now, Miss Cash, roll over and spread those legs. It's my way now.

"Yes, sir," she states, making my dick even harder.

Tinley is always a gorgeous woman, but when she has her orgasm glow, she sets me on fire. Kissing the inside of her thigh, I hear her moan as I make my way to my destination. To say that I've been thinking of this moment all day would be the truth. Honestly, I turned my normal routine upside down today because she was calling to me the second I woke up with her in my arms. So why not finish out the day the same way?

"Ryan, oh god," she says.

"Not god, kitten, but if you're good, I can make sure you reach heaven more than once tonight."

I bite down on her clit, knowing it will drive her wild and have her come off the bed. Sucking her clit, I use two fingers to pump in and out of her. The sweet taste of arousal coats my tongue, making me work her over even faster. "Tinley, are you going to come on my fingers, or do you want me to fuck you more? Tell me, kitten."

"I want you to fuck me more, Ryan. I want you to make me scream your name so that everyone knows I belong to you."

Good answer. Standing over her, I pull her again to the end of the bed so that she can see how turned on I am and watch us as she props herself up as I slowly pump in and out. As I increase my speed, she moans more a more. "That's right, Tinley, show me just how much you like my cock. How wet only I can make you and that it's only me."

I feel my balls grow tighter, and I pinch her clit as she comes on my cock, screaming my name. Then I come harder than I ever have. My vision goes blurry and my knees go weak. "Damn," is all I can say, pulling out of her once I have some feeling back in my body.

Disposing of the condom and heading back toward the bedroom, I stop at the doorway, taking in the beautiful woman in my bed, and notice that Tinley is fast asleep. I still pinch myself each day that I was lucky enough that this woman would give me a chance. Crawling into bed beside Tinley, I wrap my arms around her, breathing in her scent and kissing her neck as she sighs. A whispered phrase comes from my mouth that I'm not expecting.

"I love you, Tinley."

Chapter 17
Tinley

"I love you…" That's what came from Ryan's lips last night. Words that I didn't think would come from this man so soon. We've only been seeing each other for a few weeks. Could he really be in love with me, or was he riding the high from winning, and it just came out? The thought plays on a loop all the way back to North Carolina on Monday.

Trying not to freak out too much or become the girl who clings to each detail, I head into the one class I dread so much. One month left, that's all, then I don't have to worry about numbers again. I'm so deep in my thoughts that I don't even realize until it is too late that I smack right into a wall, but it's not a wall. It's Chase.

Looking up, I feel a bit of guilt come over me. Chase had been so sweet with the whole picture issue when it came out last month.

"My gosh, Chase. I am so, so sorry. I didn't intend to crash into you."

"It's okay, Tinley. I'm kind of glad you picked me to mow down." He laughs. "So, how have you been?" he asks, shifting on his feet a little.

I could tell he really didn't want to stay around and make small talk with me, but he was a good guy from what I had been around him, and I knew he wouldn't just turn and walk away.

"I'm good. What have you been up to?" I ask, genuinely wanting to see how he's been.

"I've been good, trying to finish my last classes before going into the real world, you know, starting my sports medicine career. I'm actually staying in Charlotte since they have all the sports and race teams," he replies quicker than I realize is possible, not wanting to make eye contact with me.

"Okay, well, have a great day. I'll see you around, Chase."

As I walk toward my class, he stops me, coming closer. "Tinley, I wanted you to know that I hope he's good to you. You're a great woman."

With a light kiss on my cheek, he walks away, leaving me with more than one thought. Ugh, what a weekend. First, Ryan saying I love you, now Chase being so sweet when I may not deserve it.

Yep, math is the bane of my existence. That was the longest hour and a half of my life. Walking to my car, my phone vibrates.

My Driver:

Hi kitten, how's the morning?

Me:

Ugh, finishing math class, why do we even need it? (frown emoji) How's your morning

My Driver:

Been in meetings about the car this morning, so its uneventful.

Me:

Wish I was with you

My Driver:

Me too, miss you. Can I call you later? I
have to stop by Brad's off before going to
the simulator to get ready for this week's
race.

Me:

Of course (kissy emoji)

My Driver:

(heart emoji)

Putting my phone back into my bag, I head home. I smile a little wider and can't wait to talk with Ryan later. Even if my stomach turns a little, I know the conversation we need to have because I have to know whether he meant those three little words or if it was just something he had said because he was so blissed out from the win and the amazing sex.

Walking into the house, I find Grace studying her phone. "Hey lady, what have you been up to? I feel like I haven't seen you in forever. What's going on?" I ask. Pausing to look at her when she still hasn't answered me. "Grace, earth to Grace, hello?" I ask again.

"What? I'm sorry," she finally says after looking up at me with a confused expression.

"Grace, what the hell, girl? What's going on?"

"Ugh, I'm sorry. I'm a little stressed about this next month, then trying to decide about the summer internship. I broke things off with Miles last week, so I'm honestly trying to figure out my next step." She finally takes a breath.

"Grace, wait back up. You broke up with Miles? But I thought you guys were in such a great place?"

"Well, we were, but then honestly, with him going into the draft with baseball and me possibly going into NASCAR and traveling, we just saw our paths going different ways and wanted to end things before we resented one another," she says with a sad but determined voice.

"Well, I'm sorry, but you may be right. He's a good guy, but I wouldn't want either of you to suffer because of work. Now answer my second question. Why were you studying your phone so hard?"

She lets out a laugh at that one. "That, my dear friend, is a story for another time. Tell me all about your weekend because the video and pictures I got told me one thing, but I want the real story from my best friend," she says, steering away from my important question.

So we spend the next hour going over my weekend in Vegas with Ryan, then the bomb dropped on me, ending with him saying, "I love you," even though he may have thought I was sleeping.

"Grace, what am I going to do? I like him so much, but am I in love? It's only been a few weeks, and it's not the normal dating life with him gone. It's more text and FaceTime, and when we have a little time that's just us, we can't seem to keep our clothes on and talk. We are making up for all the lost time, so I don't know. Could I see myself falling in love with him, yes, one hundred percent? But this little voice in my head keeps saying you better be careful, he's in the public eye, and one pretty face may turn his head."

"Tin, you need to talk with Ryan. Don't hide how you're feeling, and keep it in. He needs to know that you have doubts and fears. Who's to say that he doesn't have the same concerns, but he's in this love bubble and doesn't want to rock the boat?" Grace states.

"You're right. I'll have the adult talk, though I worry he's getting tired of hearing my worries."

Chapter 18
Ryan

"Brad, what the hell, man? Why can't you just have me on an uneventful weekend?" I say with a laugh, sitting down in the chair across from him and looking over the schedule for the upcoming race weekend.

"Well, for one, everyone wants to talk with the winner from last week's race. Another, everyone seems to love your ass. But I'm not sure why. You're not that great," he says with a laugh. "So tell me, Ryan, how was your weekend with Tinley by your side?" He gives me a smug smile.

"I'll have you know it was a great weekend." I wink at him. "Honestly, she's fit in so well with the team, travel, and the life. It's like we made it for her to be there."

"Ryan, I know you are in the great start of a relationship bubble, totally blissed out, but I want you to be very careful. Don't jump too fast." That's one thing I love most about Brad. He tells me what I need to hear, not what I want to hear. With this life, many people can turn into yes people, and I can usually spot them a mile away and try to stay clear because I don't want that on my team. So, I know if Brad is making sure I keep my feet on the ground, he's concerned.

"Thank you for your concern, Brad, but honestly, Tinley is nothing like I have ever experienced, and she may just be exactly what I need."

"Have you told her that?" he asks.

"No, but after the weekend and having her with me and a part of the team, we need to have a talk about where we are going because I'm falling hard in love with her. And I may have said it after the race, but she was asleep, so it's in the back of my head that I want to tell her sooner rather than later."

"Just be careful with not only your heart but with your head. Women can be the best thing for a driver or can be a distraction. Just find the right balance. Tinley seems like a great woman. She could care less about all the flash and celebrity, and maybe that's what you need," Brad points out.

Standing up to leave, I throw my hand up to say bye as his phone rings, so I let myself out and head down the hall to the simulator to finish my afternoon. Rounding the corner, I can hear a raised voice, and as I get closer, I notice it's coming from the sim room. "Shit, what the hell? What were you thinking? Stay focused. You don't need to be the drama. Yes, she was gorgeous, and that smart mouth turns you on, but that's it. Stay focused. Racing is the priority, not her."

Stepping into the sim lab, I see the inner monologue coming from my best friend. After how quickly he got off our phone call Sunday, I left it alone, but now I know someone has gotten under his skin. The question is, who?

"Hey man," I say as I get into the sim car to put my information in from my last run to pick up where I left off.

"Hey," he says in a clipped tone.

"Matt, what's going on with your bud? What's with the grumpiness? That's normally not your go-to. That's mine. You're the sunshine to my grumpy most weeks."

Abruptly standing, he wipes his face with this hand, looking me in the eye. I can tell something is going on, so I wait and see if he is going to say or just leave it in the air.

"It's nothing, man. I just thought something might be more than it was, is all. But looks like I'm the dumb one this time," he finally says, walking out of the room and leaving me once again with questions for my best friend.

After racing 200 laps and ensuring my car is how it needs it to be for Saturday's race, I'm ready to go home and just relax for a little while.

Me:

Hey, just leaving the shop. I'll call later.

My Girl:

That's fine, just catching up with Grace. Something odd is going on with her. I'll be around. (winkie emoji)

Me:

Weird. Matt seemed to be in a mood today also. I found him in the sim room talking to himself, and when I asked, he just mumbled and left.

My Girl:

I wonder…

Me:

Nope, not going to figure him out right now (laughing emoji)

My Girl:

okay…call me later.

Me:

I will (heart emjoi)

My Girl:

(kiss emjoi)

I arrive home a little while later. Charlotte traffic can be a bitch some days, and this was one of those. I can't help but wonder what the hell is going on with Matt. Yet again, that's in the back of my head. He's always been the level-headed one of us, never getting too wound up. The things that get under my skin, he just rolls them right off. But with our last two interactions being the way they were, I just can't let it go. Just as I'm about to make something to eat, my phone rings. Looking down, I notice it's Serena.

"Shit," I grumble. Serena was a girl I dated about a year ago. She's the opposite of Tinley; tall, blonde, and a model who's a total bitch when she's not the center of attention. That may be why we didn't work out in the long run. She was great when it was just us, but she would have that RBF firmly in place when she was with me at the track, and the attention was on me. Long story short, she moved to New York when her modeling career picked up, and that was that.

"Hello, Serena," I say, trying to sound as nice as I can on the phone.

"Ryan, hi love, I saw your win this past weekend. Amazing job," she sing-songs to me.

And that's another thing that turned me off of her. She loved when we won, but boy, did she make it known when I was racing terribly, not winning enough for her. But what she was really saying was that I didn't put her face in front of the camera enough because I was performing badly. When we were great, it was great, and the sex was always, let's just say, adventurous. But sex is only a little part of it.

"Thanks, Serena. So, to what do I owe this call?" I ask.

"Ryan, do I have to have a reason to call? Maybe I missed you and wanted to check in," she says.

"Okay, well, things are good, the team has been running

great this season, and I'm finding my grove. Getting ready for this weekend's race in Dover, Delaware."

"Aw, I thought that race was coming up. I was just thinking the other day that I would love to see you and catch up since you're going to be close to the New York area, and I could come down."

"Yeah, that will be fine. I can get you some passes if you want to come for the race this weekend," I offer, trying to be the nice guy so she will get off the phone and I can go about my night.

"Ryan, that would be so amazing! Yes, I'll be there. Can't wait to see you," she says.

"Okay, well, send me over your driver's licenses so I can get the pass and have you on the list of those okay to be around my area. I'll see you this weekend."

"See you this weekend, Ry," she says.

I can't help but clench my jaw just a little. I always hated when she called me Ry. What am I, thirteen and a girl? "Okay. Bye, Serena."

I hung up the phone. I couldn't help but have this little question in the back of my mind. Why would she call now? Had she seen the race and Tinley by my side at the winner's circle and decided I didn't need to be with someone like her? *Guess I'll find out her motive when she comes to the race this weekend.* I look down at my watch. *Shit, it's 930pm. Tinley has class tomorrow. I hope she's still awake.* Rushing to get my dinner from the fridge, I shower quickly so I can FaceTime my girl.

Chapter 19
Tinley

When 1030 pm rolls around, I'm on the verge of falling asleep. Still having heard nothing from Ryan, I'm starting to think he's not going to call. So, I go to wash my face and get ready for bed. Just as I'm getting comfy with my current Rom Com book to read just a little to calm my spinning head, my phone lights up with a FaceTime, "My Driver" on the screen. Smiling, I let it ring just a little longer than I might any other time to make him think I was sleeping. When I answer, his beautiful face comes on, wet head and all. Lordy, this man could make messy look hot any day of the week.

"I was thinking I wouldn't hear from you tonight. I was just getting ready to spend it with my latest book boyfriend," I say, a slight smirk crossing my face.

"And just who might I have competition with tonight, then, Tin?" he asks.

"Well, I'm actually reading a book about a retired navy seal protecting his fallen best friend's sister from a stalker, and it was just getting to the really spicy part where he's going on caveman over a dress she wears to the bar. So good sir, I have options," I say, laughing. Sitting back up in the bed, I notice he's also in bed. "Long day today, driver?" I ask, interested to see how the rest of the afternoon went.

"Not too terrible. Traffic was awful coming home, so that took a lot longer than normal," he said. "How was yours? Did you get any more answers out of Grace? I'm sure that girl is like a vault. The only way information comes out of her is if it is being forced out of her by three certain men." He laughs.

"Yeah, you may be right on that front. But three men, really. She doesn't even want one right now."

He chuckles. "I was talking about Jack, Jim, and Jose. You know, to have her loosen up."

Laughing at his statement, I can't help but shake my head. "You are correct about that. Those men would definitely get her talking. She did tell me she and Miles ended things. With him going into the draft and her looking at jobs with race teams to help with PR. They didn't want the pressure of being apart to mess up the friendship that they started with."

"Well, that sounds like the right move for both sides, to be honest," he says.

"What do you think of distance in our situation Tinley?" he asks, a little concern in his voice.

"Honestly, Ryan, I don't even think about it. Maybe because it's new, or maybe because I still get to see you. Don't get me wrong, it's great when I come to races with you and be by your side, but I also like my time away from all the lights and cameras. When it's just us. I know we haven't been seeing each other long, but I like the place we are in right now."

"Me too, he says. You make it easy to be myself and not put on a mask. I can just be 'Ryan,' not 'Ryan, the race car driver.'" He smiles at me.

"Well, you make it easy to be around." Laughing, I can't help but think back to the first time I laid eyes on him at the track. I thought he was this larger-than-life figure, and honestly, that would be the only time I would ever be around him. But from that first kiss, it's been something I can't put my finger on. Maybe I am falling in love. He's already said it once to me; granted, he thought I was asleep, so I know it really didn't count. But the more time I'm with him, the more my heart grows more for him.

"Tinley, where did you go just then?" I hear him ask. Blushing, I close my eyes, and when I look up at my phone, I notice Ryan has a concerned expression.

"I'm sorry," I say. "I was just thinking back to our first meeting and how far we have come in a short time. It's been a bit of a whirlwind, don't you think?"

"Well, if I'm being honest, yes, it has, but I wouldn't change anything with you, Tinley. You have turned my world on its head, and I have to say I'm enjoying it." He pauses for a second, and I think this might be the moment. He's going to tell me those words I so want to hear again, that I didn't even realize I longed to hear. But then he does something entirely different.

"What do you have going on the rest of the week?" he asks, really throwing me.

"Let's see, I've only got two weeks of classes left, so I'm just finishing up a few last-minute things for graduation and then passing the freaking math class. Again, have I told you how much I hate math?" I say with a laugh.

He chuckles again. "Yeah, you may have mentioned that once or twice." I swear his smile melts me every time I get to see it. "I better let you go, Tin. I just wanted to see your face. And Tinley....I love you," he says with a wink, and he's gone.

WTF, did the man just drop the 'I love you' bomb and hang up the phone? Sitting straight up in bed, my head is going a million miles a minute. Ryan McKenzie just said the three words every girl wants to hear, and then he hung up the phone. Letting that sit for a few seconds, I wonder if I should call him back and ask whether he actually said that. Was it a mistake, and that's why he hung up right after? I can't go to sleep after that kind of information, so I do what any normal person would do, hell I'm an adult or will be when I finish college, so they say and hit dial on his name and wait.

Chapter 20
Ryan

Yep, I've lost my mind. I just told Tinley I loved her and hung up the phone. Who does that? Well, I guess me, that's who. This woman has me under a spell where I can't see straight. I can't control my emotions and evidently cannot control what comes from my mouth. Good glory, we were just talking like a normal catch-up type of conversation, then she was thinking back to our first meeting, and the words just came out.

Letting out a groan and smacking myself in the head, I lay back in the bed. *Great job, you idiot. Just when you are getting into a great rhythm with her, and it's going the direction you want, you throw out those words.* Hell, if she runs for the hills now, I won't be surprised at all. Honestly, I would welcome that. I threw out 'I love you' and this time she was actually awake, yet I hung up the phone.

Me:

Well, I'm a dumb ass.

Matt:

Mmm gonna need more information
because that is true some days..

Me:

I may have said I love you to Tinley and
then hung up the phone.

> **Matt:**
>
> Dude, did you mean to say it?

Me:

Yeah, but just not at that moment. It just came out as we finished talking. Now I'm waiting for her to say we need to take a break.

Pacing around the room, I check my phone a few times, but the only text I have is from Matt.

> **Matt:**
>
> She may not.

Me:

Have you met me? My life is crazy, and since dating Tin, it's seemed to pick up speed.

> **Matt:**
>
> Maybe that's a good thing. She's bringing out the best in you.

Me:

Ugh, you not helping my spiral right now. Oh, and to make matters worse, Serena called me today. Maybe that's why I thought I needed to say those words.

Why the hell did I just say that? I smack myself in the forehead.

> **Matt:**

Slow the train. Serena called? Dude, that
woman is bad news, and you know it. You
think she saw you and Tinley this past
weekend and wants you back?

Me:

If she did, she said nothing, but that
wouldn't surprise me.

Matt:

Well, I don't trust that woman. She's a
snake in the grass, ready to strike. You
better watch her.

Matt was never a fan of my relationship with Serena. That
should have been my first clue that she was never a good fit for
me. When your best friend throws up red flags, that's when it's
time to cut the strings. But I was so blinded by the other stuff I
kept on going down the hill with it.

Me:

She's coming to Dover this weekend, so
heads up.

Matt:

Why would you let her around you again?

Me:

Honestly, I have no idea, but I've already
set the wheel in motion, so now I can't
take it back.

Matt:

Okay, well, back to Tin. What are you
going to do since you have basically
thrown the Love word out in the universe?

Me:

I'm just hoping it's forgotten, honestly. I
am falling in love. Who's to say she's not
also?

Matt:

Congrats, I guess then, (laughing emoji)

Me:

(facepalm emoji) Thanks, man. You have
not talked me off the ledge btw

Matt:

You're welcome. Night.

Me:

Night

Just as I set my phone down, my head still spinning, it rings.
Looking down at it, My Girl splashes across the screen.

Looks like that wasn't a dream. I said the words, and now she
calling to tell me she needs a break. "Hello," I answer.

"Umm, Ryan, did you mean what you said?" she asks.

"Hi, Tinley." I clear my throat, then do the one thing that I
have always been told to do. I tell the truth. No reason to hide
from your emotions, my mom always said. When you find the girl
that makes you want to bare your soul, it will come easy. *So then
let's see if you are correct, Mom.* I cough. "Yeah Tinley, I did. I know
it's sudden and may seem fast, but I do, and I wanted you to

know that. I completely understand if you're not in that place yet and if I scared the living hell out of you with my statement."

"Ryan, you didn't scare me at all. I love you, too. I wasn't sure if we were on that page yet. I know some men are like deer. Go slow, ya know," she said with a small laugh.

"Well, I can assure you I'm not one of those. You make me happier than I've ever been, Tin, and when I say those words, I mean them. I can tell you right now, I've never fallen head over heels in love so fast with such an amazing woman, and I wanted to spend every waking moment staring at those beautiful blue eyes."

"That's good to hear, Ryan, because, like I've said before, trust is big, but giving my heart to someone is bigger. I keep my circle small for a reason. I don't want to get hurt just because. So I'm trusting you with my heart and not to break it."

"Tinley, you have my word. I will keep your heart safe. You have mine, hell I think you had mine the first time I saw you because you took my breath away, and you have every day since then, so let me love you."

"I think I started falling the minute I ran into you and you kissed me that first time," she says.

"I'm glad you called me back. I was worried I might have scared you away by blurting that out and then just hanging up the phone."

Laughing, she says, "Well, at least I didn't say 'okay' and hand up after you said I love you. Now, that would have been a funny one to tell people," she says.

I chuckle. I can't help the smile that comes to my face.

"I'd better get to bed since it's already past midnight, and I have an early class, Ryan. I love you," she says as she gets ready to hang the phone up.

"I love you too, Tinley. Sweet dreams."

And with that, she hangs up the phone.

THE REST of the week goes faster than I could imagine. Heading toward the hanger to get on the plane, I can't help but wish that Tinley could go with me this weekend, she settles me when she is around, but part of me also wants her by my side so that Serena can see I have no interest in her and that she can march on back to New York where she belongs.

Walking onto the plane, I see Matt already sitting in his seat on his phone. Clearing my throat, he looks up and, with a shit-eating grin, asks, "So, are you single again?"

Flopping down beside him, I can't help but laugh. "You really know how to make a guy feel good this early in the morning, don't you?

"What, just asking a question? From the conversation last night, I was just waiting for you to call me back later, drowning your sorrow and saying something like, 'Matt, where did I go wrong? Why am I such a girl?'"

Punching him in the arm, I can't help but grin. "I'll have you know, smart ass, she called me back, and we talked about my, shall we call it, declaration. She said it back to me. So, there you go."

"There you go," he said.

"I have a question for you now that I have you in a metal box and you can't run from me for once. I have asked you what's going on with you twice now, and you have darted from me. So what's with the grumpy attitude this week? Each time I've seen you, you're either looking down at your phone or have a perma-nent scowl on your face."

Rolling his eyes, he turns to face me. "You're really not going to let this go, are you, man?"

"Nope," is all I say.

"Ugh, short version. I may have slept with a woman that I hate, and I do mean hate. She is bossy, smart-mouthed, and it was definitely the hottest sex of my life. Who knew that hate sex could be that good? I thought the whole point was to get it out of your system, but now I can't get her out of my thoughts. She is literally living rent-free in my head, and it's messing with my driving. It's pissing me off to the hundredth degree, okay?" he says with a huff. "Honestly, I thought that if we had sex, got it out of our system, I would be back to my normal state of mind, but no such luck. Not only have we sent some very we'll go with "fun" text, but I can't shake that this could be something, yet she makes me so crazy. If there is one thing I am not doing, it's turning me into a guy who pines after some woman who, on a good day, has a permanent scowl on her face when I'm around, amazing sex or not. So that's it. Can we stop with the therapy session now?" He finishes his rant.

"You got it, bud," I say with a grin on my face. Putting my earbuds in to listen to my playlist as the pilot tells us we are getting ready to take off.

"You got it, bud? That's all you have for me? After the information I just said?" Matt states.

I can't help but laugh at him just a little. "What? You just told me not to ask any more questions. Granted, I only asked one, and you unloaded all the information."

I can feel Matt stewing beside me, like he wants me to dig deeper, but I'm not. If he wants to tell more, he will. If not, that's okay because I know eventually, it will come out.

Me:

Taking off. Love you

My Girl:

Be safe. Love you (kiss emoji)

Putting my phone into airplane mode, I turn on my music and try to relax. But with Matt beside me, I don't know if that's possible.

Chapter 21
Ryan

Practice on Saturday is what I like to call crap. It seems like every change we make is in the opposite direction. When one part went great, another was like, nope, I'm gonna go to crap. By the time the third practice session comes around, I'm stressed out and don't want to be in the damn car anymore. John can sense that I'm getting ready to snap, so he suggests we reset the car back to square one with the track now hot from the two other sessions prior, and maybe the grip has changed the asphalt some, and it will do what we want. Or so he hopes, because if not, I just may lose my shit on this car.

Okay, let's try one more time. A frustrated breath leaves my body as I get my Hans device back on, sitting in my seat, ready to put my helmet back on.

John's voice comes over my radio as I back out to head toward the track once again. "Okay, Ryan, take it easy on the exit of turn two. That's where the issues have been. I need to see if it grips better with going back to our first setup."

"You got it, boss." I'm glad one of us has faith in this one. But I really doubt this car. My mood is getting worse with each lap. "After you exit turn four, I want you to punch it as hard as you can. I wanna test this setup hard on the next lap," he says.

"On it." As I exit the turn, I do just that. The tires grip and my adrenaline picks up. Damn, we may have found the sweet spot. Running my line around the upper side of turn one and diving into turn two, I tell John how the car is feeling and breathe a sigh of relief that we may have got it.

I hear him laughing over the mic. "You act surprised, Ryan," he says.

"Well, it's taken us all day to dial it in, so color me a little surprised, is all."

"Bring it in, and we can get the final bugs out while we still have time to work on it."

Pulling into my spot in the garage, I feel a little more at ease with the whole day, but damn, that was a hell of a start to my weekend. With the new rules, we don't always get to have practice at some tracks. It is rare we have also qualifying, so I guess it's luck that we did because if the car we started with had been the one we went out on the track Sunday with, I would have lost my shit for most of the race with the way it handled at the start of today.

Hanging my helmet inside my car, I'm just pulling myself out when I hear a yell. Turning toward the god-awful sound, I find Serena rounding the corner just as my feet hit the ground. She thrusts herself at me, and before I can react, she's kissing me. Never in my life have I ever wanted a woman off me so fast in my entire life. But she is latched onto me like the freaking spider monkey from hell. Finally, she lets up on her grip just enough for me to pull away from her as I see photographers walk away. *SHIT.*

"Serena, what the fuck are you doing?" I demand. I know my tone is a little gruffer than she's used to because she finally takes a step back from me.

"Ry, I just wanted to give you a proper hello is all. I've missed you so much, and I couldn't control myself." She steps closer to me, once again running her hand up my arm, purring a little into my ear as she does it. And that's when I hear the clicks again. The media are going to have a field day with this. I can see the headline. "Golden boy of NASCAR back with his runway girl-friend. Guess last week was just a fling."

"Serena, you have about two seconds to remove your hand from my arm before I do it for you." Not so polite.

"Ryan, I love when you talk so aggressively. It gets me so wet," she says into my ear before taking my advice and stepping back, but still in my personal space. To the naked eye, you would think we are having an intimate conversation, but to me, it's anything but that.

"What the hell are you doing here, Serena? And I want the truth, not this bullshit you are spitting about missing me and wanting to see me. Because we both know that's not true because you only have eyes for one person, and that's yourself."

"I saw your win last week, and I saw you with the frumpy-looking woman, and I just had to come see if someone like that really had your attention or if that was just some charity case you picked to be by your side for the day," she says matter-of-factly.

"Wow, Serena, you really haven't changed, have you? When you called, I thought you might have grown up, but boy, have you proved me wrong? I'll have you know that woman is the best thing that's happened to me. And honestly, she has more kindness in her little finger than I bet you have in your whole body."

"You really are with the girl? She's not even your type, Ry. I am," she whines.

Yep, I have officially tired of this conversation and this woman. What in the hell was I thinking, letting her into my life, let alone my bed, for all those months? The adventurous sex really must have clouded my judgment because, seeing her now, I can't even imagine giving her a second look.

"Ry," she says, getting closer to my ear once again. "Let me take some of that stress away from you. Just one more time. Let me touch that perfect dick. You know it will be worth it."

Click - Click - Click.

"Serena, I want you out of my garage now. I don't need your

shit, and I'm seeing someone. I don't want it. Just as I get those words out of my mouth." I see Matt come around the corner, eyes wide at the scene he's just walked in on.

Clearing his throat, he gets Serena's attention. "Hey Serena, umm, what's going on here?" he asks.

"Hey Matt, just catching up a little with Ry here." She runs her hand down my chest until she gets almost to my dick, but luckily, I'm waiting for it, jerking her wrist into my grasp.

"She was just leaving, weren't you?"

"Sure, sure. I'll go but make no mistake, Ry, this is far from over." She turns on her heel and walks away.

"What the actual fuck, man!" Matt says when she's gone from the garage. "You know Tinley is going to freak the fuck out, right? This is the one thing she was worried about, and you just confirmed it for her."

Shit. I run my hand through my hair. "I promise I did nothing. Matt, Serena came in here and basically climbed me like a tree when I got out of the car."

"Well, you better hope to god that no one got pictures of that display, or you are gonna be up shit creek with Tin. I've seen the girl be feisty with you once. If she saw you kissing another woman, I can only imagine you'll in a questionable position. She might just castrate you in front of the whole team," Matt points out.

"Let's get out of here before anything else goes the way I don't need this weekend."

Chapter 22
Tinley

"Tinley! Get your ass out here right now!" Grace calls from the living room.

"I'm coming, I'm coming, okay." This weekend may be one of my last with my girls, and evidently, I have been a bad friend since I started dating Ryan, and they are making me spend the whole weekend with them. I'm only able to check my phone once an hour while we are out, per Mia.

Stepping into the kitchen, I find Mia making drinks, and Grace has her head in her phone. Lilly is laughing at something Mia said. Grabbing Grace's phone as I pass, I say, "If I can't stay attached to my phone, then neither can you miss."

I slide over to pick up a shot Mia has ready for us. "Okay ladies, here's tonight and forgetting about anything else." The ladies all cheer. "So, what's our first adventure for the night?"

"We wanted to have dinner and then maybe head over to the dueling piano bar," Lilly says.

"That sounds perfect. I love that place. You know we always get to sing as loud as we want and no one cares when this one flashes the whole bar." I point toward Mia.

"Hey, that was pre-boyfriend. I think you ladies are on your own for flashing to get drinks tonight." Mia grins.

And with that, we all laugh as we head out the door toward the Uber and out for the fun night ahead.

"Don't stop believing. Hold on to that feeling," we sing a little louder each time the course comes around again. When we got to the bar a little over an hour ago, we were a little tipsy, and now, well, let's just say I'm glad we have the Uber app already loaded to take us home, or we would be screwed.

"Tinley, do you know how much I love you?" Grace slurs to me.

"I love you, too," I tell her, laughing as we sway.

Lilly cut us all off about three shots ago, and I'm glad because throwing up in public is not my jam. "James is going to come get us. He doesn't want us in an Uber with y'all this way," Lilly says.

"Aw," the three of us yell. "James is the best. Lilly, you better not let that one go. He's a keeper. You know, I think I have a keeper too. Did you know we said I love you this week? Yep, sure did!"

"YAY! Tin! Wait one second, that deserves a song."

Grace runs up to the piano guys and nearly faceplants it on the stage before standing up and placing her request. "Looks like we have a special request from the lovely Grace. Funny, that's your name, considering how you just came up here," the piano guy jokes. Then he plays one of my favorite country songs right now by Cole Swindell, "She had me at Heads Carolina." From the first time I heard it, it took me back to my love of Jo Dee Masina and made me smile. Singing as loud as I can, I laugh with my girls and know that this is what it's all about. I'm filled with love—for my driver, my girls, and hopefully, if things work out, I'll have the job I always wanted.

"Okay, Grace." I lean over the table so she can see I'm trying to get her to pay attention. "Why have you been so moody lately? Is it a guy? School? Or something completely different."

"Tinley, you're in love, right?" she says, slurring her words.

"You know I am."

"Why are guys such horn dogs? I met a guy, and we are so alike but so different. His body is a work of art, but when he opens his mouth, I want to stuff my underwear in it to get him quiet. Now I want the space, and he seems to have dropped feelings into the simple hookup."

"Wow, Grace, that's a lot. Who is this pain in your ass?"

"Nope, I'm not that drunk, Tin. That is going to have to wait," she says.

THE NEXT MORNING IS ROUGH. Groaning, I roll over to find I'm not alone in my bed. A grunt comes from the body beside me, and I find Grace stretched out. Laying back down, I put my foot on the floor to get the room to stop spinning once again. *Damn, what all did we drink last night?* My mouth feels like one big cotton ball, and my hair is stuck to my face. Don't get me wrong, we have tied one on before, but I couldn't tell you the last time I felt this hungover. *Note to self: do not do that again. You are too old for this shit.*

Slowly getting up to make my way to the bathroom, I glimpse at my reflection and groan again. Never again. After taking a longer-than-normal shower, I head to the kitchen to make something that will soak up all the alcohol still in my system when I notice my phone on the bar with a missed message.

My Driver:

Hi kitten, hope you had fun with the girls last night.

How had he known I was with the girls? Thinking for a second, I bet Grace told him she was keen on me not having my phone because he would not be texting and bothering us while we were out.

Me:

Good morning, my driver. I hate I didn't
get my FaceTime last night, but from what
I can remember, you wouldn't have
wanted to talk to me (Laughing emoji)

My Driver:

Really, wild night then, huh?

Me:

Let's just say I woke up with Grace in my
bed (Winking emoji)

My Driver:

I wouldn't have minded seeing that image
(Smirk emoji)

Me:

You are so funny.

My Driver:

Headed to the track. Wish me luck.

Me:

Good Luck - Love you, Be safe

My Driver:

Love you, I'll call you after. It's going to be
a busy day.

Me:

Okay, FaceTime me later (Kiss Emoji)

My Driver:

(Kiss Emoji)

Closing my phone, I start to work on breakfast. Just as I'm getting the eggs plated, I hear footsteps coming down the hall. "Please tell me you made enough for me," Grace says. Her makeup is all over, but she got her hair into a bun on the top of her head.

I hear my phone pings as I'm getting breakfast ready, but I leave it on the charge since it's almost dead.

"Of course, I made enough for you. Is Mia awake? I saw her crashed-out in your room."

"No, she's dead to the world in there. May want to leave her alone. Have you ever tried to wake her?" Grace asks. Thinking back, I think I did once she punched me in the boob. The thought sends a shiver down my spine. "I'll take that shiver you did as a yes," Grace says, laughing.

"Fair point: we will just leave her some food for when she gets up because she's gonna need it."

Sipping coffee after we finished eating, my stomach has settled, and I feel more human than I did an hour ago. "Did I almost fall in front of the whole bar last night to request a song?" Grace asks, rubbing the sides of her head.

Letting out a small laugh, I try to remember the previous night, then a lightbulb comes to me. "Yep, you sure did. That was right after I told you that Ryan said I love you."

"WHAT!" she yells, then regrets it. *Ouch.* "He told you what, when, where? Why haven't you said anything to me?"

"Whoa, slow down, tiger. It happened earlier this week."

After I tell her all about it, Grace says, "I swear, Tin, if that isn't one of the cutest things I think I've heard. So, when do you get to see him again?" she asks.

"Well, I was thinking of going to Charlotte after class on Wednesday when I'm finished for the week. That way, I can see him a few days before the Charlotte race this coming weekend."

A few hours later, I sit in front of the TV, watching all the pre-race festivity from Dover and hoping to get a small glimpse of Ryan before he gets in his car. Only to see my driver walking to his car with a long, leggy blonde draped over him. Beside him like I was only one week ago. And does he look thrilled to have her? As I sit shell-shocked, watching the show play out in front of me. Rewinding the TV back to the beginning, I watch again as Ryan and this long-legged stick walk toward his car again. Standing up, I get closer to the TV like it's going to tell me who the hell she is and why she's with him. Feeling a panic attack coming on, I reach for the arm of the chair to brace myself, feeling Grace come to stand beside me.

Rubbing my back slowly, Grace finally speaks. "Tinley, what do you need me to do? I'll help in any way I can. You just tell me."

I can literally feel my heart break into a thousand pieces the more I see the show in front of me. Why would he do this? If he loved me like he had said only a few days ago, this is one hell of a way to show it.

"Tinley, I don't want to pile onto you right now with having seen what you have play out, but you don't need to look at your computer ok, I'm warning you. My heart breaks just a little more with Grace's words. Sending him a single text, I turn my phone off to the world. The last thing I want is to see what the internet has to say about the poor girl who fell in love with the superstar only to have him play her.

Looking at my phone, I see I have a missed text from Ryan, but I'm so blinded with heart I ignore it altogether and start typing.

Me:

Why would you string me along like this?
How could you? Lose my number and
don't call me again. Have a nice time with
your model, driver. Thank you for breaking
us. You did the one thing that I told you
not to do....

Getting up from the couch, my world spins, and I don't know if I will ever be the same. Ryan took the one insecurity I told him about and just threw it in my face with no regard. How can one person literally say I love you one second, then have another woman on his arm?

Chapter 23
Ryan

I slept like shit last night. My thoughts raced with what the media would have to say with Serena appearing in the garage yesterday afternoon, and it threw my routine off this morning to get ready for the race.

"Ryan, are you up?" Brad yells.

Groaning, I roll over to get up and meet him in the living room of my bus. Damn, dude, you look like shit." He glances over at me as he sits the coffee down in front of us.

"Wow, tell me just how it is."

"Would you rather I tell you that you look amazing and race-ready? Because that, sir, would be the biggest lie I've ever told."

"Well, to what do I owe this early wake-up call?" Granted, I was already up since I got all of about two hours of sleep last night.

"Long night video chatting with Tinley?" he asks.

"Not even close. She went out with her girlfriends. However, I did get a drunken snap chat around midnight of her singing some country song Grace had requested at the bar."

"Honestly, I wanted to check in with you before you went to the track; I know Serena the snake was here yesterday, and I got to say Tin may actually kill you or, at the very least, castrate you when she wakes up from what I can only imagine was a very drunken night to see the pictures of you a Serena in the garage after final practice. It doesn't look good, man. Not at all."

I should have texted Tinley as soon as we left practice yesterday to give her a head's up about the shit storm that was going to hit this weekend would have been the stand-up thing to do. But honestly, I hadn't even figured out myself why she was here and what she wanted. I didn't want to make a big deal out of something that wasn't. The last thing I wanted was to worry her with Serena around. But I had a bad feeling about the whole thing.

I send a quick text to Tinley to try to give her a heads-up.

> My Girl:
>
> Tinley, I am so sorry so the shit storm that you may see today. Please know this is not me. I love you and would never hurt you.

Grabbing my phone, I have a ton of Google alerts with the headline "NASCAR star spotted getting cozy with ex-girlfriend super model Serena Knox after final practice."

The headlines are one thing, but the pictures are even worse. Some are of her jumping into my arms, others kissing me and speaking in my ear. My stomach turns, and I think I may be sick. Staring down at the endless messages, the one thing I worried about happening was becoming a reality. Serena came in like a bull in a china shop and just fucked my life up with one interaction. How is Tinley supposed to trust me when this happens the one weekend I travel when she's not with me?

Within 72 hours, I have gone from the happiest I've ever been to now wanting to fall into a pit and never come out. "Brad, what am I going to do? This is not what happened. Yes, she came into the garage and kissed me, but she was also told to leave me alone and get out. Tinley will not take this at face value, will she? She'll hear me out. She must. I'll spend the rest of my days making sure she knows I love her more than any race or championship could ever offer."

"Ryan, this is a lot more than just a few pictures. Serena must have been planning on you reacting the way you did. She's already issued a statement stating that you guys have been seeing each other again, and," he pauses for a second, "she's saying she's pregnant, man. That you're the father."

"WHAT! Brad, you know that that's not true. I haven't seen her in over a year and she can't be pregnant. I have been faithful to Tinley, and I always use protection."

"Ryan, what I'm getting ready to say you're not going to like, but this needs to be done today, okay, so hear me out. Taking a long breath, I brace myself for what he's going to say, but honestly, I think I really hear about half. "During the race today, I need you to look in love with Serena to make a show of it. Let her walk with you to your car, stand with you, all the things that a girlfriend or wife of a driver would do. Then first thing Monday, I am going to get the bottom of why she's throwing these claims and making a show like this," he says calmly.

"You have got to be fucking kidding me, Brad. No way in hell am I doing that. Serena has lost her mind if I will ever let her walk with me to put her hands on me. She's throwing out claims that aren't true, and we are rolling over and letting her." Getting up, I storm toward the bathroom to shower and get ready for the race.

After taking what may have been the longest shower known to man, I step out dressed to head to the track, only to be met by my best friend with an expression that I know all too well from him. "Matt, I really don't want to hear a lecture right now. I've got enough on my plate, and you, of all people, know that what is being said isn't true. I love Tinley, and I wouldn't hurt her."

"Yeah, I know you wouldn't hurt Tinley, man. And I also told you before we left Charlotte it was a bad idea to let Serena come to the track this weekend. It doesn't surprise me one bit that she would pull some shit like this. What's even worse is that Tinley is going to see those posts and messages. She's going to question everything."

"You think I don't know that? Do you think I haven't already gone over every question in my head? Brad told me yet again what they expected of me today. Serena is going to drop an even bigger bomb if I don't go out to play a happy family with her. What do I do, man? The one woman I have loved and waited for is going to be destroyed, and there is nothing I can do but get on a plane first thing tonight and grovel at her feet and hope she believes me."

Bracing my shoulder, Matt looks at me. "Listen, I know this is rough, and we both know she's lying, so why don't you call Tinley to tell her what's going on? I'm sure she will at least give you a chance to explain." I pick up my phone and dial Tinley's number, only to be met with it going straight to voicemail. My day has gone to shit, and I figure it's only going to get worse.

A few hours later, I'm headed to my car, arm-in-arm with the woman who just imploded in my life. Smiling as we walk and waving to fans, I know it's all for show, but a part of me is ready to run and never look back. Yes, I knew that being in the spotlight would hold weight, but never did I think I would be ripping my soul apart because of a job that puts me in a place of power.

"Ry, are you ready to win this one for me, for us?" Serena asks, making a show of rubbing her nonexistent bump so that the surrounding camera can get the shot they want.

Through my clenched jaw, I mutter, "In all that is holy and good, I will sort this lie out, and you will regret ever trying to fuck me over." I cup her jaw and give her a loving look so that the flashing cameras get what they want. "Now, if you will get out of my way, I need to get ready for the race," I say, not too nicely. She stops me as I turn toward my car and places a small kiss on my cheek, then walks toward Pit Road with the crew.

Never in my life have I wanted a race to be over more than

this one. Luckily for me, once I get in my car and hit the engine, all the anxiety of this morning seems to go away for a brief moment, and I'm able to focus on doing the one thing I love, driving. The car has run great, and the changes we made at practice sorted out all the mistakes.

"Ten laps to go, Ryan. I think you can push that car a little harder and get out in front. You've just been biding time the last thirty laps behind Truex," John says.

"Yeah, I think she can take the extra. Let's see if she can get around him. I catch Matt in my review as he flips me the bird before I dart in front of him, ready to make my move on Truex, but he sees me coming and blocks my advance.

"Truex will not make it easy. He wants the win and be locked into the next round. You're going to need to use Matt to slingshot you around him. Back off just a tad and lock up with him," John urges me.

Slowing my pace just enough for Matt to come up behind me, we work together to team against Truex, and when I see my opening, I shoot off like a rocket, Matt right behind me, with the white flag in the air as we come to the start/finish line.

I AM in a beyond shitty mood by the time I get back home. After returning from post-race interviews and shaking hands with everyone after the win, I'm bone tired and stressed out more than before the race. Everyone kept asking about Serena and the "baby" and if I was happy to become a dad. So, of course, I played the part and smiled the smiles so they would move along with the questions, and I could get the hell out of there. But the longer I stood and answered, the more irritated I became, and Brad could tell, so finally, he said that was all so I could make my escape. But of course, not before Serena could get one more fake moment in. Before changing to head to the plane, I turn my phone on and see the one and only text Tinley sent.

> **My Girl:**
>
> Why would you string me along like this? How could you? Lose my number and don't call me again? Have a nice time with your model, driver. Thank you for breaking us. You did the one thing that I told you not to do…

During the whole flight home, I sat and looked at her text, and now that I was home sitting on my couch, I was doing the same thing. I tried to call Tinley as soon as I got to my phone, but it was going to voicemail, which didn't surprise me, and I had left my third pathetic voicemail, hoping that I might hear from her at some point. I had thought about trying to get ahold of her through Grace but thought better of it because, well, Grace was scary on a good day, and she had already given me a very heavy warning when I showed an interest in Tinley at our very first meeting and now that this was out, she would definitively not be on my side even with this being untrue.

This was a conversation that I needed to have face-to-face. The only question was. Would she give me the time of day to have it? This was going to take a grand gesture of epic proportion to get back the girl I loved, and I would pull out all the stops. I just needed a plan.

Chapter 24
Tinley

By the time Monday rolls around, I am mentally and emotionally worn down. Every time I open my phone, I find another text or voicemail from Ryan. I just can't bring myself to listen to or even read them. I'm not ready to talk to him or hear what a fuck up he was or how sorry he is that this whole thing happened and how she meant nothing. I love you, blah, blah, blah.

"You have got to get out of this bed, Tin. You're starting to smell, and you still need to finish your last classes for this week," Mia says, jerking the covers off my body to get me up.

It hadn't taken my best friend long to see the shock on my face and see the scene playing out in front of us to know that I was destroyed. Less than forty-eight hours—that's all it took for me to go from the luckiest girl to rock bottom. "Mia, just leave me alone. I want to live in this bed."

"Nope, no can do, sister. You will not let some guy think he's won. You are going to get up, shower maybe twice, dress in a cute outfit, and go to class. So, you can either do it on your own, or I'll drag you in there and do it myself. You pick," she said.

Rolling over, I sit up, knowing good and well she would make good on the threat of washing me if I don't do it myself.

"Good girl. Now get started, and I'll find you a cute outfit to wear."

After a long ass shower, I make my way into the living room

to collect my bag and head to class. Do I feel a little better? Yeah, but I'm still heartbroken. I'm just going through the motions to appease my friends. I know they mean well, but they don't know what I am feeling or experiencing right now. I just witnessed the love of my life tell all of America he is with someone else, and she is pregnant. Pregnant! That image is still in the forefront of my head. Looking at each other and smiling, then her kissing him on the cheek as he got in the car before the race. I didn't watch the rest of the race because I'm not a total masochist.

Walking into the library, I feel eyes on me and keep my head down as I move toward a back table to sit out of sight and complete my paper for this final writing class. Just as I get all my papers out, a voice breaks through my haze.

"Hey, Tinley."

"Hey Chase, what's up?" I say, trying to sound as normal as I can.

Honestly, I just wanted to check on you. I, um, I saw yesterday's race, and I wanted to make sure that you were okay, is all."

"Oh. Okay, well, I'm fine. Thank you for asking," I tell him.

"Listen, if you need someone to talk to or just a person to sit with, let me know. I know we may not know each other that well, but my offer still stands."

"Thank you, Chase. That's really sweet of you, but honestly, I just want to be alone. Really, I kind of got myself into the spot, so I don't blame anyone but myself. I should have listened to my gut and went with the safer option of what I had in front of me."

"Well, I hope that option would have been me because, Tin, I could honestly say that I would have treated you the way you deserved and not made you look like the girl that came between old lovers who now are going to have a kid, but I do get it and I still want to be your friend," Chase said.

"I know that Chase and maybe I would have chosen differently in another life, but I just want to be by myself for now." I try to not sound like a total bitch in the process but my give a shit meter is tapped out at the moment.

"Okay, well, like I said, text or call if you change your mind." Bending down, he kisses me on the cheek and walks away. Ugh, what the hell? Chase is so sweet and so nice to me, but I stepped outside my world and jumped. Now I'm sitting here broken and putting pieces back together alone.

After finishing up classes, I head home. Pulling into the driveway of the house, I notice a dodge charger only I don't recognize it. Slowly getting out of the car, I hear shouting coming from inside, so I hurry up the stairs to see what the hell is happening.

"You have a lot of fucking nerve coming here for your scum bag of a buddy!" I hear Grace shout as I open the door, soon followed by a book being thrown toward a ducking Matt. If this whole thing wasn't such a mess it might be a little hilarious watching this tall blond specimen of a man dodging books being hurled at him.

"Have you lost your ever-loving mind, Red? I'm not here for him. I'm here to check on Tinley. So will you stop fucking throwing books at me?" Matt says.

"I want you out of this house. She's got nothing to say to you, and especially not to him."

"Well, that's for her to decide," walking into the room a little farther now that Grace has ceased fire on Matt.

"Matt, what are you doing here?" I ask, stepping closer now so they know that I'm in the room.

"I needed to see if you were okay after the shit storm that was this weekend, and I knew you wouldn't talk to me over the phone."

"Well, as you can see, I'm not okay, so you can run back to Ryan and tell him. Then, while you're at it, tell him to take a long walk off a short cliff."

"Tinley, I'm not here for him, I promise," he says.

"Like I said, I'm not fine. But I blame myself for it also."

I pass by him, heading to my room, and close the door. I sit staring at the fan, going around for what feels like forever until I hear Matt's charger start up, and Grace comes into my room shortly after.

"You know you didn't have to go all crazy lady on Matt, Grace," I say as she comes to sit beside me.

"Yeah, I know I didn't have to, but Ryan wasn't here, so I just picked the next best thing: Matt." She lets out a laugh. "Tinley, time for honesty. Matt told me what happened this weekend with that horrible woman, Serena. After I finally calmed down enough to listen to him. And I think you need to hear Ryan out. He's really devastated about all this. I know I'm not the one who is normally the tender-hearted friend, and I would gladly castrate him myself if I had even the slightest thought, he might have done something like this to hurt you, but I've seen y'all together, and I don't see it in his nature to just go so public to embarrass you or hurt you this much."

"But how can I trust him, Grace? The one thing I told him I was so worried about happened. He knew I was so nervous about going public with our relationship and me being the opposite of that woman, and he just stomped on it with a Barbie-wannabe ex, who is now carrying his child," I say as tears fall once again.

"I know, Tin. I get that, but if you're really done with Ryan, doesn't he deserve to tell you his side before you write him off?" she asks.

Maybe she's right about hearing Ryan out and finding out what's true and what's just the media. Looking down at my phone, I decide to listen to the voicemails he left.

VM:

Tinley, it's me. Please call me back. We
need to talk. I love you.

.   .   .

VW:

I know you have seen the news by now,
or someone has told you. Please call me.
It's not true, and I need you to hear it from
me. Please. I love you.

VW:

This is my final voicemail. I know you
don't want to talk to me, and I get it. I do.
But you know I wouldn't do anything to
hurt you, Tin. You're my heart, and it will
only ever be yours. This has gotten out of
hand, and Serena is lying to everyone.
Please call me back. I need to see you. I
love you, always and forever.

TEARS FALL as I play the final voicemail over again, trying to wrap my head around what he said. She's lying. Why would someone lie about being pregnant? What is the reason she would destroy us that way?

F ive days, five long days. That's how long I have sat by the phone waiting for a message from Tinley. I went silent after leaving three voicemails and more text messages than I can count. Matt came by late Tuesday to let me know he had gone to talk to Tinley and explain the situation but was met by Grace throwing books at his head and then Tinley dismissing him. He told Grace everything, hoping that maybe she could get Tinley to talk to me, but so far, nothing.

"Hey man," I hear Matt call out from the door. "Shit, bud, have you been on the couch since I left you Tuesday?"

"Yep," is all I say. Every time I went into my bedroom, all I could see was Tinley, her perfect body in my bed, her smell on my pillow from the shampoo she used. So after the first night back, I slept on the couch instead of punishing myself even more than I was already doing.

"You need to get your ass up. We have to get to the race shop; you haven't been in all week, and the race is this weekend," Matt says.

"Yeah, I know we have a race, but that is honestly the last place I want to be right now."

Coming over to sit near me, Matt pulls me up and shoves me toward my bathroom just as a knock at my door makes my heart rate pick up. Could she be here, wanting to hear the truth, talk to me, and be back in my arms?

"Ry, are you here?"

"What the fuck do you want, Serena? Haven't you done enough damage in this lifetime?" I ask, ready to fight like hell with her now that we aren't in front of the public eye.

"Whoa, bud. Calm down. You don't want her twisting something even more if you lose your shit on her, okay." Matt says, trying to get me back in check.

"Serena, why are you here?" I ask, calmer, but not by much.

"Ry, now that's no way to talk to the mother of your child, now, is it?"

"We have no child Serena; I haven't been with you in over a year, and you know it. So why don't you save me the dramatics? There aren't cameras here for you to play up to. What do you really want from me?"

"Just what I deserve. You threw me away without a second thought. I really thought we had something great, but the second another girl turned your head, I was out like last week's trash. So when I saw you with the frumpy-looking girl at Vegas, I knew I could get you back. There was no way you would be with someone like that compared to me."

"Don't you dare talk about Tinley. She has more class in her little finger than you ever will."

Serena cackles. "You really are living in a fantasy, aren't you?" she says, stepping closer to me. "You think she will last in this world? At your side? They will eat her up and spit out. They will make her life a living hell in the media, and she won't survive it. Mark my words, I did her a favor with my little, as you call it, stunt.

"What makes you so sure about that?"

Hearing the front door slam pulls my attention from the shit show that has turned into my life, and I see Tinley come into view. I'm blown away by how beautiful she is; her dark hair curled just how I always love it. She wears a pair of jeans that hang her curvy body and those blue eyes that have the fire of an active volcano shooting daggers at Serena.

"Who says you get to be judge, jury, and executioner in my life? I've lasted in your world, as you call it, for a few months now without judgment or the mean girls' club. And believe me when I tell you, you don't want to mess with my mean girls' side because I may look all sweet and innocent but mark my words, I will go to hell and back for the ones I love. Now," she says, flicking Serena's forehead, "I think it's time you and I had a little talk, don't you… Selena, is it?"

"It's Serena, actually, and you must be the homewrecker," she spits.

"Let's chat, shall we? And you can tell me just how far along you are and when this all happened. I'd like to have all the facts straight before I just bow out and call a spade a spade with this relationship, if you don't mind."

"If you must know, it happened around six months ago, one drunken night with Ryan, and let me tell you, it was very memorable, she said, rubbing her nonexistent bump."

Don't get me wrong, I know most new moms start to have one, but you would think a model as tiny as she would have a noticeable one, Tinley thinks.

"Well, that's funny considering he's never mentioned seeing you recently and said that you guys had broken up over a year ago but do continue this is rather interesting. Do you have any pictures of the little one? I know new moms always want to show off those little blob pictures. Care to show those?"

"Well, I don't have one on me," she says.

"You come into town like a tornado ripping up everything, but you have no proof? I am shocked." I clutch my necklace like a true Southern belle. "Well, I'll tell you what, let's go right now. With all your and Ryan's connections around town, we should have no trouble finding someone to get us a picture of the little one, considering you are so far along. Isn't that right?"

I look her dead in the eye, seeing the moment she realizes I've won. That I played dirty and won. For once, the nerd beat the prom queen, and I'm going to just sit back and watch what happens next.

"Go on, Serena, tell the class what's the truth now, or we can go find someone to take an ultrasound of you and confirm what I think," I say ever so sweetly.

She jumps to her feet and lunges at me. "You bitch!" she shouts. "You just couldn't leave him alone, could you? He's mine."

I block her punch aimed at me. "No, I couldn't because there is one thing that I know: Ryan is a good man. He would never leave someone when they needed him. Especially if they were pregnant with his child. But for a person to use being pregnant to try a worm back into someone's life, that's where I draw the line. Millions of women struggle each day with pregnancy and loss, and you, dear, are not about to make light of that just to make him take you back. He doesn't want you. Get over it!"

"Serena, I want you to leave now!" Ryan shouts, "You will hear from my lawyer, so you might as well get one for yourself."

Turning on her heels, she storms out of the room. Just like that, the curvy girl broke the evil model in the room.

"Tinley, what are you doing here?" I ask, not wanting to sound like a dick.

Tinley looks up from the floor, finally meeting my gaze.

"When Matt came to our house the other day and spoke with Grace, I didn't want to hear what he had to say. I was too in my head, not wanting to hear him out. I finally let Grace tell me what Matt had to say, and I couldn't stand not talking with you face to face. So here I am. Guess I just picked the right moment to come in. Sorry if I interrupted something, but I couldn't hold back when I saw her here."

"Kitten, I've missed you." I reach for her hand, turning her to see her face. Those beautiful blue eyes hold every doubt, fear, and worry I've had about talking with her for the last five days in them. She's broken, and I did that. I made her second-guess me and my love for her.

"Tinley, I am so sorry. I promise I did not know she would go to such great lengths to get me back, and that she would make a scene at the race saying we were having a baby." I want to be completely honest with her while she's willing to hear me out. I'm ready to lay my heart on the line for this beautiful woman.

I walk us toward the couch, motioning for her to have a seat. Blowing out a small breath, I start from the beginning. "She called me last week. Serena wanted to see me while we were at the race since it was within driving distance of New York. But I swear to you, I didn't know she had this elaborate plan to make it look like she was having my child and that we were seeing one another again."

"Ryan, why didn't you tell me you had talked to her? I don't care that she called. The part that hurts is that you felt you didn't need to tell me that an old girlfriend was coming to see you."

"I know, pretty girl, and I will regret not telling you until my last breath. When we were together, everyone always told me she was just using me to help her modeling career, but I was so in the middle of it that I didn't see what was going on. I should have known she might pull a stunt like this. She never wanted to be a part of my world. She only wanted the fame and notoriety that came with it." I cup her face in my hands, wanting to make sure she hears the next part and doesn't doubt me.

"Tinley Cash, I LOVE YOU; I love you more than NASCAR, more than my next breath. You are my entire world. I don't want to lose what we have because it has been the best time in my life, and you make me want to give you the entire world. And I will if you will let me."

Chapter 26
Tinley

Tears stream down my face as I listen to Ryan pour his heart out to me. I wanted to hear those words and for him to make me feel safe again. With Serena standing in the living room, I knew I could not hold my tongue, so I unleashed on her. She had no right to think Ryan would ever want to be with someone like her.

I move to straddle Ryan's lap. I want to be closer to him, to feel his body against mine. This man owns me, and I'm going to make damn sure he knows just how I feel. All I want in this moment is to kiss him. But I know we needed to get every sentence.

"Ryan, I love you too. I have waited what feels like a lifetime for you. I know that your life is in the media; I get that. But I also know that your life outside of that world is just as important. I want to be the one you come home to. The one that you tell all your darkest secrets. I want to stand beside you every time you get into that car and go to work."

"Tinley having you with me is all I have ever wanted. You complete me and make me a better man. So, if you will still have me, you have all of me. Know that I may not always be the best, but I will always give one thousand percent to us."

With tears streaming down my face once again, I can't help but smile at the amazing man in front of me and wonder just how lucky I am that I get to go on this amazing journey with him. We may have started off in an unconventional manner, but this man stole my heart from the moment I literally ran into him. Looking back, I think he took my breath away when I watched him interact with the young girl and her father asking for an autograph that very first day.

"I can't wait to see what the future may hold for us. I love you, Ryan McKenzie."

4 Days Later……..

"Oh god, yes, yes, Ryan, yes."

"That's right, Tinley, tell me just how wet you are. Tell me you want my cock inside you and that mine is the only one you will ever want."

"Yes, Ryan, fuck me now, it's you. It's only ever been you." Thrusting inside her as hard as I can, I let out a moan at how tight she is. Waking up on race day, there is no better feeling than knowing she's right beside me. We haven't been apart since we laid everything out on the line a few days ago.

"Fuck Ryan, I'm close."

"I know, kitten."

I pinch her clit. She goes over the edge, tightening around me, and I feel my release right behind her, thrusting into her two more times. I groan her name, and my release rocks me so hard my knees go weak.

"Damn kitten, I have missed you." With a small laugh, she smacks my arm to get me to lie down beside her.

"You know I have to be on the track in less than an hour, kitten."

"Ugh, stay with me." She moans, stroking my already hard cock. Ready to go once again.

"You're going to kill me, Tinley. If I'm worn out, I can't win today and then see my beautiful girl in the victory circle."

"Well, we can't have that now, can we?" she says sweetly.

Kissing her one more time, I make myself get out of bed to shower and head toward the garage, where I bet John is already pacing the floor because I'm usually already checking over my car one last time before the race. Yet here I am, having a hard time leaving this beautiful woman in my bed. As I exit the bathroom, I find Tinley curled up in front of the TV watching Race Day Live. Just as I come into the room, I see why she's watching it with so much interest. They are discussing the drama that is my life right now. When Serena left my house that night, I called Brad as soon as I finished talking with Tinley and filled him in on everything that Tinley had gotten out of her. He set the rest in motion. Making sure that my lawyer was aware of what she had said. She stated that she was pregnant with my child and that I had been seeing Tinley behind her back, or at least that was one story I had seen. Now the press was doing an about-face and telling my side.

"Hi, kitten," I said, kissing the side of her head.

"Hi, love," she says. Taking her eyes off the TV to look up at me with those ice-blue eyes I fell in love with all those months ago.

"Okay, I better get going, or I'm going to miss the drivers' meeting, and if that happens, it's a serious fine, and I don't want to worry about points being taken from me because I miss the meeting. But I'll see you beside my car later, right?"

"Of course. Wouldn't miss it for the world."

"Okay, love you."

"Love you too."

Pulling into the racetrack, and a zip of excitement comes over me. This time last week, I dreaded being at the track. Serena had made my life hell, and the media were relentless with questions. But after the last few days since the statement was put out, I can breathe a little easier.

"It's about time you showed up, bud," John says as I make my way down to the row. He's sitting, waiting for the meeting to start.

"Yeah, yeah, I know I'm late."

"Hey, I'm just glad you are here. I'd hate to replace you when we are running so good. Wait, could that smile be because a certain curvy brunette is back in your life?" he asks.

Smirking as I face forward. "Well, if you must know, yes. Tinley gave this sorry S.O.B. another shot. I intend to make up for lost time."

"Wow, man, you are so whipped."

I can't help but laugh at how crazy that sounds, but how right it sounds as well.

Following the drivers' meeting, I head to the garage with John to make sure everything is good for today. Since I missed my morning planning session with him, it's the least I can do.

Three hours later, standing by my car, the national anthem plays, and this beautiful girl is by my side. I can't help but think how grateful I am to do what I love.

If you had told me six months ago, I would stand beside the love of my life. I would have told you to fuck off. But here I am, and hopefully, I'll soon be asking Tinley to be my wife.

"Okay, my driver, time to go to work," Tinley says, kissing me. "I have something for you. Since the last time I gave you this, you won, I thought it was only fitting to give another," she says with a wink, placing that single penny into my hand once again. I'll see you after the race. I love you."

And with that, I strap into my seat and watch as the love of my life goes to the pit area.

Some say that life is made up of core memories that shape us as we go. That they make us into the people we are destined to be. With Tinley, she became a core memory the moment I saw her shy nature talking with Grace. The way she carried herself and didn't make a show of being someone she wasn't. She became my Driving Force and the love of my life.

Epilogue

2 Years Later

"Your 2025 NASCAR Cup Series Champion is Ryan McKenzie."

Walking out onto stage, I can't help but be taken aback just a little. This is my life. This is what I have been working towards since I became a driver. I have worked my ass off to prove that I deserve to be here. Looking out over the audience, I notice my friends and family stand cheering, but the one person I seek, the one who always makes my palms sweat and heart race, is sitting, tears streaming down her face at how proud she is of me rubbing her very pregnant belly. We got married a little over a year ago, and not long after, she told me she was pregnant. Looking at the due dates, I wondered if she would make it to this day, but being the team player she is, she made sure that our little one knew mommy needed to be at the important day for me for us.

Just as I step up to the podium to thank those more important around me, I notice my mom go to sit beside Tinley. My heart speeds just a little, noticing she's rocking back and forth. Trying to get through my speech just a little quicker than I know I should I keep my eye on my beautiful wife. Just as I finish my speech, I hear her say, "Oh God."

And just like that, I'm in protective mode. "Again, thank you to NASCAR for giving me honor of being the 2025 Champion. If you will excuse me, my wife seems to have gone into labor while I've been up here talking, so I'm going to leave to get her to the hospital, cheers everyone," I say with a small laugh trying not to panic in front of the entire NASCAR community, because inside I'm flipping out.

Tinley

4 Days after the NASCAR Awards Banquet.

"Ryan, you need to come back to bed," I say, watching my sexy husband as he stands by our son's crib.

"I know, but I can't believe this beautiful little boy is ours," he says.

After twelve hours of labor, our son came into this world kicking and screaming all the way. Landry James McKenzie. Having his father's hair and my blue eyes. He's the perfect mix of us both.

Never in my wildest dreams did I think I could love someone as much as I love Ryan, but the second they placed Landry into my arms, my heart grew even more in that instant. Getting Ryan's attention once again, I motion for him to follow me.

"Let him sleep. He's going to be up in a few hours, and I sure would like just a little time with my husband before that happens," I say, laughing.

Ryan walks toward me, wrapping his hands around my back and pulling me close. Walking us back toward our bedroom. "You know what I really want I can't have for eight weeks," he says, kissing me with as much passion as the first time.

Cupping his already hard dick, I can't help but be turned on. Groaning, he pulls back just enough so that I can see his eyes are trained on me. "Tinley, you are playing with fire here."

Maybe I like that, I say, dropping to my knees and kissing as I go. "I know you may not give me what I want because of this rule after giving birth to our son, but I can give you what you want." Releasing his already hard cock, I smirk up at him as I slowly take him into my mouth. Hearing him moan is the best feeling, and I know I'm driving him crazy.

"Damn kitten, you are so good at that. I swear I'm gonna come so hard, please don't stop" he said. Sucking faster, I cup his balls, pulling just a little like I know drives him wide. He groans one more time before he spills down my throat.

"Shit, Tinley, shit, that was so good."

Standing up, I kiss him, letting him taste just how much I enjoyed pleasing him. "You know that as soon as I can, I'm putting another baby in that belly of yours." Laughing, she looks at me with more love than I can ever imagine deserving. "Thank you, Tinley."

Looking at me like I've lost my mind, she says, "What are you thanking me for?"

"For picking me, making me your husband, and now a dad. You gave me a life I never thought I wanted or need. If my racing career ended tomorrow, I would still be the luckiest guy in the world, and that's all because you gave me that chance. I love you."

THE END

Want more Matt & Grace continue reading for a sneak peek.

PreOrder Now Driving Wild

Matt & Grace's story coming next year.

Grace

Deep breath, I do not need a man in my life to define me, holding back tears I sit in Ryan McKenzie's racing hauler waiting for him and my best friend, Tinley, to return from victory lane. I have loved watching them fall in love, but it also reminds me that I just pulled the pin on my own happily ever after and blew it away.

But Miles and my lives were going in different directions. Baseball is the one thing my ex-boyfriend has always wanted, and I'm determined to make a name for myself in the stock car world. Hopefully as the up-and-coming Mac Motorsports PR person. I just can't stand the idea we would grow too resent each other if it became his career or mine. He was drafted by his top choice and heading to AAA ball, he wants me to follow him around the minors. I'm too strong of a woman to sit by and let that be everything I am in life.

Taking another sip of my Diet Coke I'm hit with the realization my relationships aren't the defining factor of who I am. I will not rely on a man because I am independent and don't need one. I'm going to move on from what I thought might be the love of my life. And I know just who I need to set my sights on to get over my old love. Because everyone knows the best way to get over someone is to get under someone else.

"Grace, are you still here?" Tinley asks as she comes up the stairs into the hauler.

"Yeah, I'm here," I say throwing my can in the trash. "Are you ready to head back to Boone?"

The way she quickly looks to the ground and scuffs her shoe, has me betting the answer is no.

"Well, would you be okay if Matt took you back? I'd like to stay with Ryan since he won, and we want to celebrate a little bit." A shy smile lifts her lips.

Tinley & Ryan are so sickly cute and into one another that it makes my heart feel great for them. She's always been the quiet one of our group, so when the hot playboy of NASCAR took an interest in her it was such a great boost to her self-esteem, and I am loving seeing this new Tinley emerge.

It doesn't hurt that Ryan has a hot-as-sin best friend for me to look at. He's perfection until he opens his mouth. The things that man says get under my skin and piss me off anytime we're together. Granted that southern accent he hits you with makes the words sound pretty, even if they annoy the hell out of me. I never knew it was possible to simultaneously want someone and want to strangle them.

Granted the last time we were alone I was throwing books at his head, but that's a story for another day.

"It's okay, I can just drive back, and Ryan can bring you home. I don't need Matt." I shrug as I stand to leave. Just as I close the door on the hauler, I run into the person who Tinley was just talking about. Did she just Beetlejuice this man?

"Ouch." I slam into his hard chest and the smell of motor oil hits my nose. "Oh, hey Matt."

Friendly. Just be friendly, yet the way my heart picks up just a little when his eyes land on me.

"Yeah, hey Red. Is Ryan in his trailer?" he asks his eyes taking me in. Those blues of his are something a girl could get used to.

"Where else would he be, Cowboy, it is HIS trailer?" I

answer, with a little sass, not really caring for the nickname he's given me. "But he's a little busy with Tin."

"Figures, I have a shitty race and need to talk, and once again he's too busy." His tone is more aggressive than I think is fair.

But trying to be a good friend to Tinley and get along with this man, I reply, "Anything I can do to help? I might not know all that he does about cars, but I'm a good listener."

"Sure, come onto the hauler, and you can listen to me bitch and moan about my day. Or we can do something else. Talking isn't my usual go-to after a shit day." Matt's sweet southern drawl makes me shiver as he rubs a hand through his blond hair and sends me a wink.

Shrugging I think to myself. *Why not, turns out I'm driving myself home tonight, so what's the rush I guess? This sexy driver might be just what I need to get over Miles.*

"Okay, well come on, I need a beer among other things," he says giving me a lust-filled rake of his eyes over my body one last time before turning to walk toward his hauler.

I may not care for his fuck anything that comes to him mentality, but I could do with a release.

When we make it to where he's parked, my body is on fire from the looks that he's sending my way alone. Yet between him being on the phone and the grumble of a conversation that I can barely make out with Ryan, I am already over his mood and need a stiff drink.

Walking onto his hauler it has the same layout as Ryan's, the small living area and kitchen are set up as a mirror image but the colors are just a little different. It is surprisingly clean considering the rumors about Matt being the party racing guy. And having a different girl at each track. You know the frat boy mentality. Granted the life he may lead really isn't made for having a girlfriend.

"Nice place," I say, trying to start a little bit of conversation as I look around.

"Want a beer, Red? I've got some of those White Claws you drink. Tinley made sure that I stock them since she and Ryan are attached at the hip now," he says.

"That would be great, thanks. But make sure I only have this one." Taking the drink, I settle on the couch across from him.

"So, were you hiding out in the hauler during the race, or did you actually watch it this time?" he asks.

"You keeping tabs on me, Cowboy?"

"Just trying to make small talk, considering this is the first time we've had a conversation alone, I'm trying to figure you out."

"Well, if you really want to know, I was with Brad for most of the race going over some PR items for the week that he asked for my help on."

"Guess my poor performance and wreck will be on that list of items to talk about, especially since I didn't play the nicest when talking with the media after the race."

"Yeah, your name did come up." Taking a sip of my drink I look over at him.

"So, tell me, Red, why the sudden interest in wanting to talk? You've made it clear that I'm just a fuckboy, your words, not mine. Granted, I will say I like sex as much as the next guy." You made it clear that I was only good for one thing and that I wouldn't be anywhere near that. Sting with a smirk.

Every wonder that it would like to be another person for a night. Always having to play the part that everyone expects of you. Maybe we can do something a little reckless for just one night.

Setting my drink down I go to settle in his lap. Rubbing my breast up against his hard-muscled chest, it's difficult not to want to grind on him, but I restrain myself for the moment.

"I tell you what, Cowboy, how about tonight we get what we really want out of one another and skip the chit-chat?" I propose and start to remove my shirt leaving me in just a lacy bra.

"You've been craving getting me under you and don't deny it because your buddy already told on you." I rub myself over him, feeling just how turned on he is already.

"Shit, Red." He moves his hips in just the right motion to make me moan from the contact.

"Why do you call me that?" I ask really wanting to know the reason he's settled on that nickname.

Lifting his hand to my neck he rubs slowly. "I call you Red because of this beautiful smart-ass mouth of yours. You don't know how long I've thought about you on your knees with those full red lips wrapped around me and you moaning my name" He continues making his way down my neck to my breast.

"Do you know how long I've wanted these tits in my mouth" He unhooks the front clasp of my bra exposing me. After a groan, he takes one of my nipples causing more moans to slip from me.

"Tell me what you want, Red. You want me to fuck you into oblivion because I can, or you want to just grind down on me like a couple of high school kids because I can promise I'll make that just as good," he asks before taking my other breast in his mouth making me even wetter.

"I want you to fuck me so hard that it'll make me wonder why I hate you so much," I whimper rubbing my hot sex over his already hard erection.

It only takes a second to get the words out then he's on his feet and my legs are wrapped around his waist while he walks toward the bed.

"Strip now, Red, I wanna see what's hiding underneath the rest of those clothes. Those tits are perfect, I can only imagine that your pussy is even better," he groans, his eyes darkening with lust.

Slowly removing my jeans and my lace thong, I'm left bare for him. Then he takes his time walking around me as if I'm a picture hanging on the wall. Just when I think he's going to say something about me standing here, he slaps my ass with such force that I bend over the end of the bed and let out a gasp.

"I knew you'd like a little kink, Red; you just need the right person to give it to you." he whispers into my ear leaning over my back, making me shiver.

"Then what are you waiting for, Cowboy? I want you to fuck me, not stand around and ahhhhh." I don't even get my sentence out, and he slams into me, sending me forward. And because I've turned into a needy little slut, I moan louder than ever before. He works me over so quickly, winding me up with just the perfect pace.

"Oh my god, yes. Harder!" I demand.

"You like me being rough, Red. Do you like it when a man pulls on this blonde hair and fucks you harder?" he seethes.

"Yes, don't stop, punish me, Cowboy. I've been a bad girl," I moan.

Who the hell is this woman right now, I don't let a man control sex, I'm the one who is dominant. Yet of course with Matt I want to be dirty and let *him* have the power, I want him to do things I've only seen in porn movies. This man has been a pain in my ass for the last few months, yet here I am, moaning and dripping wet for him. I've officially catapulted into another universe.

"Now you're going to be a good girl for me and come when I say, aren't you, Grace?" I hear Matt ask; the low timbre of his voice makes my sex clench even more.

"If you wanted a good girl then you should have found a pit lizard, Cowboy, because I don't follow the rules that easily," I sass him, earning me a smack on my ass.

Pulling out, Matt stands behind me, "You wanna be a brat then?" he asks.

Looking over my shoulder, I say, "They do have so much more fun, don't you think?"

I watch as Matt moves to sit at the head of the bed. Rubbing my thighs together because, yep, I've turned into that needy little slut he thinks I am.

"You want to be a brat and not do what I ask, then you can ride me, and don't you dare play with yourself while you're standing there," he grouches.

With a smirk and a slow glance up his body, I enjoy the view before crawling toward him. I'm going to enjoy this torture more than he knows. Two can play this game.

Just as I'm getting to his perfect, and I do mean perfect, dick, I stop to give it a small pump just to drive him a little crazy.

"Red, you either suck my dick or ride it. I'm only going to say it once." That deep southern drawl comes out even more now that he's turned on, and it makes my sex clench even more. Damn, that's hot. I do love a Southern man.

"Oh, I'm going to ride you." I look up into those gorgeous blue eyes that are almost black, filled with lust. "Because this will be your only time to get this perfect pussy around your cock," I counter with a smirk as I slowly ease onto his dick.

Finally, I take him in as far as I can. Moving up and down, adjusting to his size, and getting into a rhythm. I move my hips to just the right spot so that I know I'm driving him just as wild as it's making me.

"Damn, Red, you're so wet for me, look at how easily you're taking my dick," he utters before sucking my breast and biting my nipple, sending another tremor through my body.

"Yes, yes, yes." Throwing my head back and giving him better access to what I know he wants more of, I pick up speed as he bites my other nipple and sucks it into his mouth.

Feeling my legs start to shake and sparks spread through my body, I let out a moan just before seeing stars. "I'm coming, Matt, yes, god yes, I'm coming," I scream just as I feel him pulse inside me releasing a groan as I hear my name slip from his lips.

Coming down from my orgasm, I sit up on the bed just as I see Matt come out of the bathroom.

"Damn, Red, I knew you'd be a firecracker but didn't think you'd like it rough."

Leaning against the door, I can't help but marvel at the beautifully arrogant man in front of me. If only he didn't piss me off with opening his mouth, I could go for a repeat. He knows just how to make my body sing. Looking up at him again, that V will be my downfall If I ever give in to him again. Matt lives up to his fuckboy good time, I'll give him that, but it was also just what I needed to move on and that's all this was.

Getting off the bed in search of my clothes, I give him a little smirk as I bend to pick up my lace panties, jeans, and top.

"This was fun, Cowboy. Thanks, I needed that." I fix my hair and then blow him a kiss while I head toward the door.

With one more look at that gorgeous body and the man who gets under my skin daily, I close the door. Leaving Matt and that chapter of my life in my rear view because that's just where Matt should stay. Or so I thought.

(STAY TUNED for this Frenemies to Lovers coming March 2024, these two are just getting started)

PreOrder Now Driving Wild

DRIVING SERIES

Ryan & Tinley's Story

Order Now:

Driving Force

Matt & Grace's Story is coming early next year.

PreOrder Now:

Driving Wild

The final book in the driving series will be out

Late Fall. Wonder who this couple

will be follow along for details.

PreOrder Now:

Driving with Heart

Acknowledgments

WOW, who would have guessed I would have completed this book. Honestly, not me haha. This book came as a little spark in my head when covid hit and I was home with my kids trying to help with schoolwork. I found out quickly they did not intend me to be a teacher, nor was I one in a previous life. But hey, they made it through, and I got a book idea out of it.

To my husband, thank you for helping with the NASCAR bits. I know you thought I was crazy when I asked questions about the track or what the pit crew side of things but hey, it helped.

To Jenni Bara, thank you for working with me on this book as I went. Helping me find spots that needed more or didn't need as much. When we started I didn't think this book would ever get to the point of publishing it, but you pushed me and told me I could do it, and that helped to have you in my corner. And don't worry, just because this book is done, I'm still not quitting my PA job, so you're still going to be stuck with me.

To Annie Charme, thank you for reading over my words and helping with scenes that needed just a little more. An answering all my publishing questions I had leading up to this moment.

Too Emily Silver, thank you for your friendship and for reading over my words. Having you in my corner has been such a great and positive experience. From the first time I bugged you with me reading your words, I told you that you were stuck with me, and guess what? Now you are. An I am so honored to call you a friend.

To Cadwallader Photography, thank you so much for the beautiful image and for helping pick the one that worked perfectly. And Aaron Wolber for being the face of Ryan McKenzie. Thank you for being a part of this process and being so sweet when I know I messaged you asking for videos haha. So here's to the next two coming down the line soon.

To Samantha with Sammie Bee Designs for bringing my cover to life. Who would have ever imagined being a reader that one day I would ask you to bring my cover design to life? I couldn't have asked for a better partner in this adventure and both covers are beyond anything I could have ask for.

To Kate Seger, thank you so much for putting up with me and editing my story. You make me a better writer. I'm so glad you took a chance on my writing.

To the readers… thank you for taking the time to read my story. Being a reader first, I know you have so many options on what to read; if you choose mine, I am forever grateful. I know the story may not be perfect but for a first time author I'm so glad you wanted to read it.

Becoming a writer wasn't something on my radar, but I just started writing. This book has been a work of love and patience, and I'm so glad that the words finally came together, and you have them in your hands now. Enjoy!!

Haley

About the Author

Hi everyone, I'm Haley (some of you may know me as The Southern Librarian in the book community) …. Married to my best friend and mother of two teen boys. I grew up in small town North Carolina and still live there now.

Racing has been in my blood my whole life, my dad taught me how to count using race cars and then going to tracks when I was a little girl. To meeting my husband at a local dirt track. So, it's easy to see that I would write a NASCAR trope.

Stay tuned for what's to come and I hope you enjoy this ride with me.